Disintegrate

A novel by
Neil Godbout

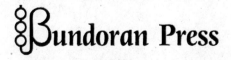
Bundoran Press

Cover Illustration: Heidi Martinson
Cover Design: Virginia O'Dine

Printed in Canada
Published by Bundoran Press Publishing House
www.bundoranpress.com

Library and Archives Canada Cataloguing in Publication

Godbout, Neil, 1968-
    Disintegrate / Neil Godbout.
(The broken guardian series)\

ISBN 978-0-9782052-8-7
    I. Title. II. Series: Godbout, Neil, 1968- . Broken guardian series.
PS8613.O298D58 2011   jC813'.6   C2011-904965-1

Bundoran Press gratefully acknowledges the support of the Province of British Columbia through the British Columbia Arts Council.

The Broken Guardian Series

Disintegrate
Dissolve

Claire Godbout – lead guitar
Shelley St. Amand – rhythm guitar
Kieran Hoekstra – piano
Mari Martin – bass
Virginia O'Dine – synthesizers
Nathalie Mallet – French horn
Michelle Read – acoustic guitar
Betsy Trumpener - mandolin
Grace Flack – saxophone
Patty Stewart – pedal steel guitar
Lisa Martinson – cello
Rachel Huston – violin
Ronda Krafta – backing vocals
Walter Beardwood, Gord Hoekstra, Rodney Venis - horns

First mix - Mari Martin
Final mix, engineering - Virginia O'Dine

The Good Lad
Brodie Sawatsky
Dec. 27, 1997 – Dec. 3, 2010

Black spot on the sun (Amara)

I see you, Sam.

I have stood outside your window and watched you every night while you sleep from the day you were born.

Your parents may have fed you and bathed you and nurtured you but I made you.

I sculpted you. I constructed you.

And now, more than 17 years later, on this day, you will meet your target.

I have set a series of events into motion.

On this day, you will meet her.

The trap will be sprung.

Good.

Meet and Greet (Sam)

"Cindy, you are such a slut."

The girl who just called Cindy a slut lets the screen door slam shut and bounces down the two steps. I hear her strange goodbye while on the sidewalk, a quick silent moment between songs on my MP3 player. I am about to walk by, slightly ahead of her. The next song starts, something quiet, so I hear her voice again.

"Hey. Can you hear me?"

I stop awkwardly, half-tripping on the sidewalk. I look to her face, startled. She smirks at me and taps her ear.

"Oh."

I pull the earbuds out and stuff them into my pocket. I can hear the guitars starting to buzz angrily in my jeans.

"Are you heading to school?" she asks.

"Um…yeah."

"Can I walk with you? I'm new."

"Uh…yeah, sure."

She comes up to me.

"I'm Lily. I'm starting Grade 12."

"Hi." My voice is a little too high in my ears for my liking. Nice one. New girl introduces herself, you introduce yourself as the soprano in the choir.

"I'm Sam. I'm in Grade 12, too."

Better.

Now start walking with the nice girl on the first day of school.

My feet begin to move. She joins me.

"Do you live near here?" Her voice has this calm, mature confidence to it, experienced at making conversation with new people or calling Cindy a slut.

The voice is smooth and cool, like how I remembered Dad pressing the ice pack firmly against my ankle after I had turned it playing soccer for the Orchard City Spartans when I was 10.

Yet the insult hadn't been mean. It was stating the obvious, as if both of them – the girl moving through the doorway saying it and the unseen Cindy inside the house – knew it was true.

She also seems comfortable with me right away. I have that effect on girls, Pete always says. They want you like an old shoe, buddy, but they don't want to be seen in public wearing you.

"The next block over, on Woodlawn," I answer, ignoring Pete's voice in my head. I'll be hearing him soon enough and our new Miss Lily will quickly forget my name.

"Have you lived here long?"

"Born here."

"That's perfect luck. So you know everyone and can introduce me." Her voice tinkles like she has found a dollar on the ground.

"Yeah, sure."

"If that's okay with you."

"Oh, yeah, sure. That's cool."

"First days are so hard. I didn't want to leave the year before graduation but Cindy got this great opportunity here so I didn't have a choice."

"Where are you from?"

"Vancouver."

Sophisticated city girl comes to small town Kelowna. Meets born-and-raised local yokel. Sounds happily-ever-after.

"So what do you think of Kelowna?" I ask and immediately cringe. Nice question, Mr. Suave. Why don't you ask her what she thinks of your Old Spice underarm deodorant?

"It's nice," she says, smiling and looking over at me, catching my eye. "I like the scenery."

"Yeah," I say, looking up to the street and beyond to the mountains across the lake in the distance. "It's pretty cool."

Wait a second. What the—?

Is she flirting with me?

She doesn't have glasses so it can't be blindness. Didn't think girls from Vancouver were so polite. What can she be seeing? The mirror this morning had told me the same sad story it has repeated all through high school. Stringy brown hair that hangs lifelessly against my head, surrounding a face that continues to lose too many acne battles. The smile is good and so are the brown eyes, or at least Kathy says so, but the hawk nose ruins the party. Although I'm nearly six feet tall, my thin body still looks boyish. More meat, more bread, put some man on those bones, Dad thumps me on the back. I love his encouragement. It fills me with confidence and pride. I always tell him that. Too bad your sarcasm developed before the rest of you, he answers back.

Got me there, Dad. Right in the heart.

"So what does K.L.O. stand for?" she asks as a few cars speed by on K.L.O. Road. I recognize Mr. Jacobs's black coupe. If the guys at our school aren't hot enough for her, there's the algebra teacher, Mr. Jacobs. He always draws an estrogen crowd during track season in the spring when he does wind sprints without a shirt on with Pete and the other naturally gifted athletes.

"Kelowna Land and Orchard," I recite. "I guess the old people couldn't think of a name for the street."

"Or the school," she chuckles.

We wait at the corner for the light to change, K.L.O. High School sitting on the other side of the street, a scruffy collection of grey buildings surrounded by yellow grass, burned by the summer sun. There are already more than a hundred people hanging around the front doors. Nobody wants to go inside. The sun shines warm and a soft breeze blows, carrying this light scent into my face.

I breathe deeply and hold it. It's a sweet smell but not

sugary. Deeper. It makes me think of Pete's older sister, Pam, who is in third year of university in Vancouver. I have known her all of my life so I remember her as a little girl, a willing extra player on our baseball team on spring nights in the park. Now she's a woman, so far above us, so smart and sophisticated and beyond me. It's a rich smell, like how girls…no, not girls—women—should smell. Mature. Confident. Captivating. Like that substitute teacher we had a few times in Grade 6 or Jason Buckhorn's mom.

It's coming from her.

It's coming from Lily.

The light changes but I don't move. I am desperately trying to get to the surface, to clear that intoxicating smell from my brain.

She moves and takes her scent with her. I quickly fall into step, confused. I'm not a perfume guy, especially since most of the school girls wear it by the gallon, stinking of vanilla fudge bars that have been baked in bug repellant. This isn't like that. It was there and now it's gone but it still echoes in my sinuses.

"You okay, Sam? Seems like you're the nervous one, instead of me."

"Oh, no. No. Just distracted. Well…" We're coming up to the curb. I can see Pete near the door, enclosed by four giggly younger girls, flashing his smile. Kathy is coming down the sidewalk from the other direction, her face brightening as she sees me. She will be with us in a minute.

"Listen…um… This is going to sound real dorky… but that's an amazing perfume you're wearing." I manage to get out the last words before running out of breath. My face is already turning hot. I consider stopping to wait in the street so that the approaching pickup can make me a big bloody decoration on its front grille. Well, at least I won't have to introduce her all day. She's going to run away screaming right now.

She turns to me as we step up on the curb. She looks shocked for just a flash of a second. Her eyes widen and her mouth droops, like I've told her she forgot to put a shirt on before she left the house. She recovers quickly. She bathes me in a warm smile, her lips pulling up around her perfect teeth. Her eyes are still surprised.

"What a nice thing to say. Thank you, Sam. You're so kind to notice."

"Yeah, sure."

I look up and Kathy is there.

"Hey, Kathy. This is Lily. She's new. She just lives a block down from me. She's going to be in our grad class with us."

Kathy being Kathy gushes welcome and the girls are chattering away like sisters in seconds. I follow them onto the grass towards the doors. Pete shakes off his adoring fan club and falls into step with me.

"Hey, buddy. Who's the sweetheart? And how come she's with you?"

"Thanks for the pep talk. She's the new girl. Her name is Lily. And I'm sure she'll forget she ever met me as soon as I introduce her to you."

"Right you are, buddy," he says, grinning and slapping my back.

"…and you'll love the mall, I'll take you there later if you want, if you haven't been there already…" Kathy is at full-speed now. It's time to let her take a breath but Pete beats me to the punch.

"Yeah, I'm sure Lily has seen a mall before, Kathy,"

Pete booms, too harshly. Kathy stops cold but her face is red with embarrassment. She looks away.

Pete holds out his big, rough hand to Lily, a broad smile across his face, his icy blue eyes intent on her. He's giving her the full Pete treatment, the you-don't-need-to-know-any-other-guys-at-this-school-now-that-you-know-me hurricane.

Lily meets his hand and they shake quickly.

"Hi, Pete." Before he can start on his smooth speech, she's already turning back to Kathy.

"I'd love to go the mall, Kathy. How about this week-end? I didn't get a chance to do much shopping with the move and everything."

Lily starts moving away with Kathy.

"Oh, Sam." Lily turns back to me and put her fingers on my elbow lightly. "Would you walk me to the office? I still have to register."

Her touch is a booster cable, its current moving my feet towards the doors as the bell sounds and a collective groan from the gathered students meets it.

"See you later, Kathy," Lily sings over her shoulder.

"Nice meeting you, Paul," she adds back at Pete in that same chilled tone I had heard her first use at her house when I first saw her.

Paul, who started the morning as Sweet Pete, the muf-fin man all the girls love, stands still. Principal's honour roll list every semester, captain of the volleyball team, lead saxophone player in the band, best friend since pre-school, Pete is not used to the brush off. He catches my eye.

"Paul?" he mouths, his face wondering when he sud-denly transformed into dog food.

I turn back to Lily, beaming. Back to school, my ass.

This is already the best morning in months. New girl smells great and flirts with me, then takes my friend's never-fail come-on and walks all over it.

"That's Pete, actually," I say, not trying very hard to hide a chuckle.

"Oh, I know, Sam," she says quietly, leaning towards me as we slow at the doors. "I just don't like boys who expect girls to worship them."

"Yeah, sure. Me, neither. I mean, I don't like boys… uh, yeah."

She smiles and I hold the doors, thinking shutting up was the best approach for now.

I drop Lily off with Mrs. Cambridge at the office, she of the horn-rimmed glasses and permanent scowl.

"Sorry, I have to run. I need to find out where my classes are."

"I'm sure you'll find me later."

"Yeah," I say, looking into her smiling face. "Sure, I'll track you down."

I hustle down the hallway, nodding to the familiar faces and mumbling hi to the rest.

"Hey, Sam. Wait up." Pete's right behind me.

"Oh, hey, Paul. How was your summer? Impress any new girls lately, Paul?" I can't remember Pete ever having struck out with a girl so bad so I'm going to get as many laughs out of it as I can before Lily comes to her senses.

"Nice," he says, shaking his head in disgust. "The hottest girl to show up at this school in, like, ever, and Pete falls out of the blocks."

"I hadn't noticed."

Pete, a great guy but the conversation always has a way of being about him, thinks I mean how he had tripped up on the introductions. He starts all indignant about how

Lily got off on the wrong foot, she's just nervous, or maybe stupid. I make noise in all the right places to keep him going on his rant but I'm not listening.

What I hadn't noticed was Lily being hot. I actually can't picture her at all, even though I left her less than a minute ago. I can see the smile and those rich green eyes but that's all, except for that perfume. I still feel half-drunk from it. It smells dangerous but somehow knowing. A smell that could get me into a lot of trouble and I wouldn't care. I breathe deeply and sigh without thinking.

"Hey, am I boring you?" Pete complains as we reach the door to Mrs. Tilton's class. "And you can wipe that stupid smile off your face anytime. She's just using you to show me up. She'll come around."

"Do really think she's that hot?" I ask as we take seats in the half-full class.

"Smoking, buddy." He chucks his pen and it hits me in the side of the head. "Get some glasses."

"She smells great," I reply, picking up Pete's pen and flipping it back to him.

"Ok, then," Pete says, making a face.

Mrs. Tilton hands out some worn paperback copies of Hamlet and begins talking about Shakespeare's great tragedy. I read the play over the summer so I snag some brownie points by raising my hand and adding a few thoughts. Mrs. Tilton smiles at me. As soon as she turns back to the board, I get the pen in the side of my head again.

"Suck."

This time, I just smile and leave the pen on the floor.

*When the angels came, there was only the
  screaming.
The people wailed,
Clawing at their faces, ripping their skin.
The angels smiled, pleased.
Parents admiring their babies.*

Outrageous fortune (Sam)

Lily is waiting for me at my locker at lunch, although I don't see her right away. As I approach, I wonder why everyone is slowing down and staring at my locker as they walk by. Then I clue in. Lily is getting the "new girl" examination. It seems she's passing. Most of the guys are giving her the full-body scan while the girls are sizing up a new potential threat.

Her face lights up when she sees me and those lush green eyes shine, high beams to go with the smile.

I look at her closely as I smile back in recognition, trying to see what Pete and everyone else but me seems to see.

She has dark brown hair, cut in this modern pixie style around her small ears. She has no earrings. She wears this plain oversized white dress shirt, a guy's shirt, with the sleeves rolled up to her elbows and these funky beach capris with ballet flats. She is average height. She isn't thin but she isn't a big girl, either. Ordinary, in a nice way, is the best way I can describe her, yet there is something fascinating and unique. She is her own person, immune to social pressures. Who doesn't want to stand next to a person like that?

"So how was your morning?" I ask, stopping in front of my locker.

"Fantastic," she grins. "I'm already in the yearbook club, the prom organizing committee and I got elected to grad council."

"Whoa," I reply, finishing with the combination and opening my locker.

A notebook falls to the floor, pushed out of the top shelf. I had stuffed all of my year's school supplies and other crap from my backpack inside during the break. Lily bends down quickly to pick it up. The notebook has nothing written on the cover, not even my name, but it is well used. Anyone could tell at a glance it isn't new.

"What class have you had that you've done so much writing already?" she asks, opening the book.

"Wait.. don't…" I cry, too loud. A few heads turn as other students walk by. Lily looks up, not startled but curious. Then she glances back at the page.

For anyone else, I would have ripped the book from their hands before letting them read what's inside. I would have run to the janitor's room and swallowed every drop of cleaning fluid if Pete ever got his grubby jock mitts on that and he's my best friend. Kathy knows the book exists but is a good enough friend to not ask about what's inside. I've always dreaded something like this might happen but I keep the notebook with me, especially at school. Some of my best ideas happen here, daydreaming in class. I can't keep them in my head long enough to wait until I get home.

So I stand there nervously. I bite the corner of my lip and look around to make sure we don't have an audience. Pete must be outside, surrounded by his cult of young girls, boosting his confidence for another run at Lily. Kathy is working at the lunch counter. Any glances this way are not at me or my notebook but at the girl holding it. She seems oblivious to the attention.

Lily even makes a half-motion to hand it back and then stops. Now she is holding it with both hands and not scanning, but reading. I don't want to make a scene but I want that book back. I sigh, turning to my locker, grabbing a juice box, a squashed peanut butter sandwich and a banana before slamming the door shut and snapping the lock in place.

She doesn't get the hint. Worse. Now she is leafing through the notebook, lingering over the words.

"Lily." I say as quietly but firmly as I can. I hold out my hand for the book.

"Just one more minute, Sam," she looks up for an instant. "I like this."

"But—"

"Sshhhhhhhhhh…"

She lingers on the sound, letting the gentle hiss slowly fade from her lips, like she is soothing a baby. Her left hand has come up from the notebook, forefinger just inches from my mouth to silence me. A quick waft of that perfume follows and I take a deep breath.

If trust and feeling safe and calmness and serenity have a smell, this is it. I can feel myself relaxing, my heart slowing down from its anxious state as Lily skims quickly to the last page of writing. She closes it slowly. She hands it back to me, staring into my eyes. Her smile is soft with understanding.

"This is some pretty powerful stuff," she says as I take the notebook gently out of her hands, as if it will fall apart if I don't hold it carefully. I pull it up against my side, unconsciously protective.

"You are full of surprises, Sam I-don't-even-know-what-your-last-name-is."

She smiles again.

"Gardner," I say, studying her face closely for any sign of sarcasm. This isn't what I expected from anyone who would have gone through the notebook.

"Of course," her smile broadens.

"Of course what?" I ask suspiciously.

"Nothing," she says, shaking her head and chuckling softly. "Your name fits you."

She looks at my face again and sees the uncertainty.

"Sam Gardner," she says, her voice becoming low and serious. She steps closer, putting her hand on my bare arm, near the notebook. She stares intently into my eyes. "You are a harvester of ideas and unseen realities in the rich loam of your imagination, far beyond mundane experience. You tend to your visions in the hothouse of your mind, eager to see them grow and evolve. You have no idea how far this gift could take you, away from this existence, into the beyond."

I blink rapidly, trying to understand what she is saying.

An echo of a smile moves across her mouth.

"Your secret is safe with me."

She backs away and turns to go.

"I want to sign up as a library assistant and I need to get my books for my next class. Walk me home after school?" Her voice is back up to its bright tone.

"Yeah, sure." My throat feels dry and the words seem to be trying to come out through a mouthful of gauze.

"See you then." Her voice chimes and she is heading down the hall.

I stare after her. I can only remember a few of the words she said just a few seconds ago. Harvester. Loam. Visions. Gift. Beyond.

Seventeen-year-old girls don't speak that way, even the ones from Vancouver, using words like that.

The feeling the words left behind is washing over me. She spent a short minute looking through my notebook and somehow saw past the ridiculous words. Lily saw what I saw. She understood. She felt the effort and the emotion. She isn't afraid. She had looked behind the curtain and she liked what she saw.

Or am I fooling myself, tricking myself into believing someone I didn't even know could get all the ridiculous thoughts spinning in the back of my head without killing themselves laughing? I doubted anyone could look at my notebook without wondering whether I belong on the psychiatric ward, loaded with drugs. I feel violated, like she has pulled away the thick veil I keep over my face to hide my true self. She was so casual about something so private. I should be furious but her words and reaction dampened any anger I might have had.

I squeeze the notebook closer. I want to lock it away or burn it. Before I can figure out which, a heavy hand slaps me on the shoulder.

"Now do you see what I mean?" Pete's brash voice is close to my ear.

"Look at the girl's back end and tell me you don't think she's hot."

Lily is still in sight of us, about to turn the corner towards the library.

"Yeah," I gasp. "Yeah, sure."

If hot means burning like the sun overhead, seeing everything, as you stand in the desert with no place to hide.

The rest of the day goes by quickly, same old school crap. Unlike Pete, I have to work at school to get my grades, which still aren't as good as his. I enjoy school, more than I want to admit. I'm not popular like Pete or admired like Kathy for her kindness and generosity. I float along on the edges. I know everyone but outside of Pete and Kathy, I don't really have friends. Kathy, in her sweet way, is always encouraging and sympathetic, while Pete, in his not-so-sweet way, is consistently disparaging. I guess the two of them both tell me what I want to hear.

Kathy stops me in the hall on the way to history class.

"Lily is so cool. We're going to the mall and a movie on Saturday. Do you want to come?"

"Yeah, sure." I mumble.

Kathy scowls at my less than enthusiastic reply.

I try again, with feeling, this time tacking on a smile.

"That'd be great. Thanks for asking."

She brightens at this and scoots off down the hall.

Story of my life right there.

Two girls going shopping. Invite Sam to carry the bags and pretend to care about the clothes and the other junk they'll buy, smile as they giggle over every little observation they make, pretend not to hear as they ogle some guy folding shirts in a men's clothing store. Worse yet, get dragged into the men's store on the premise they see something I'll look good in but they really want a closer look at the pretty boy.

The only good store in the mall is Ted's comic book shop, tucked into the corner by the back entrance. I worked there the last two summers and old Ted wants me to take some weekend shifts now that school is back in session. He says I'm a dedicated employee with good knowledge of the product.

"Yeah, sure," I laughed back at Ted when he told me that. "Call me when you need me."

Ted and I both know the truth, of course. He gave

me a T-shirt after I was done working for him the summer before that perfectly summed up our professional relationship. It said "Will work for comic books" on the front. Whatever pay Ted gave me went straight back into his pocket, after I settled my tab.

I wore the shirt in June when I went in to see if I could get another job over the summer with him.

"Sam, this year I will actually pay you," he answered.

Sure enough, even though I spent this summer plowing all of my proceeds back into his store, he gave me a $500 bonus last weekend.

"Great job this summer, kid" he barked, trying to be like J. Jonah Jameson. "Go spend this somewhere else. Your money is no good here."

"Thanks, Ted. You don't have to."

"Yeah, whatever," he said, turning away. The old softie got all emotional. Ted loves all the kids, virtually all boys but a few girls, who have come into his shop over the years, getting their superhero fix. The back wall of his office is filled with photos from former regulars and summer employees who have gone on to college and work and families and careers. Some of them still come in, having graduated to graphic novels about mice surviving the Holocaust and stuff like that.

He was acting busy with a lunch box display I had arranged that morning.

"So you'll work Thursday nights and all day Sunday this year?"

"Yeah, sure."

Well, at least I'd have an excuse to ditch the Lily and Kathy shopping extravaganza Saturday if it went too late. Sam's a working man and he's got a Sunday job. Sorry, ladies.

I'm telling myself as I head back to my locker after the final bell that I will only spend my Thursday night proceeds on comics while saving my Sunday pay. I pull open the squeaky door and frown. My notebook…I grab it and stuff it roughly into my backpack, angry with myself again for letting it fall into Lily's hands. I'm also mad that I'm not as angry as I should be. She seems genuinely interested in my poems and stuff but she has already shown herself to be ridiculously polite. Still, I'm not going to be testing her patience again. Out of sight, out of mind from her curious eyes, I think, as I pile my homework on top of the notebook.

Those strange words she said are still bouncing around the inside of my head. The only reason I know the definition of loam was I found it when looking in the thesaurus for another word for soil for a poem I did. I wonder if she is quoting from something. That's the only explanation I can come up with. Nobody talks like that.

And then her perfume is here again, scrubbing from my mind her words and comic books and homework and everything else I'm thinking about. I breathe, drawing that scent in deeply. It smells like lying naked in silk sheets, or at least what I think that would feel like, since I've never done that before. Smooth and sinful and indulgent.

I push my face into my locker to escape, jarring myself back to life with the rude smells of sweaty gym strip, old textbooks and the new plastic odour of binders and a backpack bought a few days earlier.

"See something in there you like or are you trying to hide from me?" Lily's voice chirps behind me.

Startled, I turn my head as I step back. First my jaw and then my nose slams hard into the metal frame.

"Unh."

I stand there, stunned. If life's a cartoon, there are little yellow birdies flying around my head, singing joyfully.

Lily's looking down the hall, pretending she hasn't seen the collision between my face and the side of my locker.

"Have you ever noticed that high schools in real life don't look anything like the ones on TV? The real ones are dirtier and darker."

"Yeah, sure," I say automatically.

"So, are you ready to walk me home, Sam?" She turns back to me and smiles.

In the end, we begged for death,
Begged for freedom from our agony
Begged for escape from our crimes
They smiled, cutting through us with their
  eyes
They saw us for what we were
Blindly scrambling for another moment of life.
Their wings gently stirred
Fanning the flames.

Out of my head (Lily)

I close the front door and race over to the window so I can see Sam as he walks down the street towards his home.

He stops to put his ear buds in so he can listen to his music.

Now he is walking again.

I turn away, shaking my head.

What a fool I am.

I spoke to him in my true voice.
He heard it.
Why did I take such a risk?
What am I thinking?
Cindy will be furious so I must not tell her.
I read his writing.
He senses all of us.
He knows.
But he is beautiful.
I do not want to have to kill him.
Not again.

Playtime (Amara)

Cherry and Ruby inform me that the meeting took place but I was already conscious of it.

I felt the dormant awareness I had carefully implanted within my Samael stir.

I have to grit my teeth to avoid the temptation of him because Lily will sense me and this moment I have so carefully prepared will be lost.

I tell Cherry and Ruby to cease their future observations.

Lilith and Cindy must feel safe.

Their guard must be down when Samael is unveiled.

I drag my fingernails down the side of my face but not hard enough to tear the skin.

To be free from this shape and this place will be a blessing.

In his head (Lily)·

Before I met this Sam, before I murdered Samael,

before the humans and life in the universe, before the other guardians, and even before Cindy, I was there. In the nothingness of the before, there was a yearning and I was born in that yearning. And in the instant of creation, as the universe sprang from the void, before the other guardians emerged, Cindy was there.

We are two as one—I am the yearning and Cindy is the consummation of the yearning; the desire made flesh. And there is the wanting for more, always more, and the circle is complete.

When the first stars and systems and galaxies were ready to die, Cindy and I understood. We watched the death guardian claim them, extinguishing their light, and we knew there was an exit to this place. Most of the other guardians refuse to accept this outcome, to see the end of things. They chose to see transformations from one state to another. They invented change and the progression of the universe, evolving over the expanse of time. Nothing ever dies, they argue, especially us. We are the building blocks of existence, the caretakers of this place. We are essential to the continuation of the universe. The shape and motion and action of all things flowed through us.

Sam is touching me in his dreams and he is starting to see me and the rest of us.

He should not be doing that.

I should not be here.

I run away.

Out of my head (Sam)

The dreams start that night and there is no escape.

Lily's scent is coming off everyone as I walk through a city. That perfume radiates off the skin of everyone I pass. Like an animal, the smell tells me different things.

That man in a suit smells like he wants power so bad, he would kill for it. The younger man walking with him craves money, more money.

In the alley, two men are slumped against a wall. One craves a big enough score that he can finally kill himself. The other wants his children to forgive him and he doesn't know how to ask.

Inside a coffee shop, a woman in her early thirties is hoping she can have kids. The girl in university working behind the counter wants to get a research grant so she can tell her boss what he can do with his coffee beans.

Lily is everywhere but I can't find her. The more I breathe in her scent, the more I know about the hidden desires of everyone around me and the closer I feel to her. She must be close but why can't I see her?

Everyone wants something but it's all the same. They just want control, over themselves and over everyone else. They all want to escape from where they are. They want someone or something they don't have.

They are so pathetic, with their sad cravings for power and money and time and quiet and satisfaction.

There's a teenage boy sitting on a bench, his dark hair hanging down into his face as he writes feverishly into a book. The desire just pours off him in waves, so thick I can barely breathe. He wants so bad to be noticed, wants to write something pure and timeless and perfect, wants to tap into something bigger than himself, wants everyone to recognize his incredible insight, his blinding intelligence.

I always wake up in the dark after I see myself on the bench. Sometimes I feel so small and sad and empty that I bite the sheets so I don't cry.

Soap (Sam)

Pete comes by Saturday after lunch to play some video games.

"So are you and Lily together or what?" he blurts out as I hand him his controller.

"Ummm…no, man. I don't think so. We walk together to school and back. That's it."

"Right."

We get our weapons and start shooting at the zombies. Except for some grunts and curses at the screen, we're quiet.

"So, that's okay if I keep making my move," he says, between levels, eyes on the screen, not looking at me.

I hit the pause button and look at Pete, smirking.

"Whoa… Hold on here. Are you asking my permission? Is the great Pete, oh charming one, sweet lover of the ladies, man amongst boys, hunkolicious—"

Still not looking at me, he frowns and flips up his middle finger.

"—hunter of womanhood, are you asking me if Lily is fair game?"

"I'll take all that crap coming out of your mouth as a yes," he says, a slow smile now spreading on his face.

"She still not giving you the time of day, huh?"

"The only guys she talks to are the math and science dweebs, the acting class goofs and you. She must be one of those girls who's hot for nerds."

"Well, she hasn't exactly put the moves on me," I slump into the couch and stare at the TV. The screen is frozen at the start of level six. The zombies will come from behind the wall on the left to start.

"See, that's your problem, my man Sam," Pete sits

up, animated now that we're talking about my pathetic record with the ladies. "You sit there waiting for the girls to come to you. Be a man. Pluck the fruit from the tree."

I snort and click the game back on.

We play for another half an hour but now I'm distracted. I'm trying to figure out how to get rid of Pete. I have to drive over to pick up Kathy and Lily soon so I can chaperone their shopping and movie date.

"Are you getting changed or what?" he says, putting down his controller and checking his watch. He just lost the last of his lives. I still have three more.

"What?"

"I'm not going out on some stupid girl double date crap with you if you're going to look like that."

"You're—what?—date?"

"Jeez, you look so sexy when you're confused, man. Why don't you go take your monthly shower and put on some clothes that weren't handed down to you from your dad? Introduce yourself to a comb. Lily asked me if I would take her and Kathy to the mall." He rolls his eyes. "Didn't tell me I had to babysit you until after I said yes."

"Oh, yeah, sure. The girls. Right."

Pete gets up.

"I'm going to grab a Coke and give my sympathy to your mom. How could such a smart lady raise such a tool?"

I grab his controller, throw it with mine in a drawer and shut the game and the TV off.

"Yeah, sure," I grumble, getting up. "Go remind my mom why I should be more like you. Don't forget to give some love to Sara."

"Man, that's your sister you're pimping and she's in Grade 7," he protests as I leave the room.

Sara's a sore spot with Pete. She's adored him since before she was in kindergarten. In the last year, the adoration from Sara has evolved into outright unashamed flirtation. Pete isn't cool with a little girl still in elementary school batting her eyes at him and hanging onto his every word, sighing stupidly.

I chuck my T-shirt and sweats into a dark corner of my bedroom, throw on a robe and dart into the bathroom. As I start the water running, I wonder what the girls are up to.

Did Kathy plan this to get closer to Pete? She's crazy for that big goof, when he's so clearly not her type. She even went out with some teammate of his from the basketball team last year just to be closer to Pete, then abruptly broke it off when she realized how cruel that was. Poor Tommy Bricker never knew what hit him. She digs me, she digs me not.

I think Kathy's kinda cute, although she hates it when I tell her that. She has long and thick reddish blonde hair with light freckles on her face, neck and arms. She's shorter than most of the girls but has a bigger personality. She's a take-charge kind of girl, but in a nice way, in a let-me-make-our-lives-better kind of way. She's always bringing people together to do stuff, whether it's serving lunch at school or raising money for animals at the SPCA or taking the new girl out to the mall.

Sometimes I fool myself and think that Kathy would be good for me. I like the idea of holding her close to me but then I remember that Kathy's eyes see Pete only. Instead, I just sit around at her house, watching movies until late or we walk together by the lake, sharing our little secrets and fears.

For some reason, I think Lily has more to do with today's festivities than Kathy. Making such a blatant move towards Pete isn't Kathy's style. Lily seems much more direct. Is she trying to set them up? Or did she invite Pete for herself, not knowing how Kathy feels? Is Lily just playing tough to get with Pete?

Okay, Days Of Our Lives, get out of the shower, I tell myself, turning the water off.

When the disease finally got to me,
Most of them were already dead.
I had listened to their frail moans for weeks,
Watching the sickness eat them from the in-
side.
In the streets, the angels walked through the
blood,
Nothing on their faces but the Mona Lisa.

Making connections (Lily)

I look at myself in the mirror and I like what I see.

I am not Cindy, of course, but I am passably attractive.

In my human form, which I have worn almost without interruption for more than 3,000 years, I am a 17-year-old girl. I have no more choice in my physical form than any other guardian. This is my shape. Bodie told me that our human form is a reflection of our guardian selves somehow.

I stare at my face and I see what he means. I see Lily, a girl on the cusp of being a woman, but never arriving, never leaving that limbo between the innocence and energy of childhood and the sad maturity of the adult human experience. I am nothing but potential.

Potential is nothing without the prospect of fulfillment

and I am the opposite of fulfillment. I can only want.

So I am nothing.

I want to be human so much.

I am so tired of taking their form. I want to be one of them.

Humanity is Cindy's greatest creation—a species that looks like us and thinks like us. They are weak and fragile and short-lived but they can reproduce, a power we lack. They are as curious as we are about their origins and their role. Their scientists are actively looking at us, although their methods and logic examines only the footprints of guardians, not the guardians themselves. The only ones who can see us are the visionaries, the prophets, the artists, the writers, the delusional, the insane, depending on the culture. They tell stories and draw pictures and write songs about us. We are written into their myths of creation and salvation.

I wonder if Sam will be different from the others. Can he see me and stay himself?

We are going on a date, the four of us.

I have quickly immersed myself into the culture of this school.

I am having fun.

I should be excited but I am anxious.

I have not told Cindy about Sam so I will be watching both her and him closely.

Will Sam sense her?

Will he sense me?

Will Cindy recognize the threat?

I want a no to all these questions but I am foolish.

Making connections (Sam)

Pete and I stand just inside the front entrance of Orchard Park, trying to look bored and not like we're waiting for anyone. I'm looking at the front display of the bookstore. Pete's playing with his cell phone. The mall's busy with Saturday afternoon shoppers.

As usual, the air conditioning in the mall is jacked up so I feel the sudden change in temperature right away. It isn't as if somebody is holding the door open for their grandpa in a wheelchair. The Kelowna heat, even in September, is dry background noise. This warmth I feel right now is like stepping in a sauna and throwing some water on the rocks. It's steamy, moving stealthily into the sinuses and lungs. I feel lost, like something's out of balance. The warmth is filling my head and making my brain slow and dull.

Before I can look around to find out where this blast of heat is coming from, I catch Lily's scent. I close my eyes and pull it into me, covering myself with it like I have been outside for hours shoveling snow in January and now I'm back inside with a thick blanket. It seems even richer than ever today, fuller. If a smell could be happy and content with itself, it's this. Blissful and serene.

Instead of the front entrance, where Pete is impatiently staring, I look the other way, down into the mall, expecting Lily to be nearby. I blink twice, startled. She has just come around the corner, still mostly hidden, blocked by the bustle of shoppers, at least a hundred feet away. Kathy is to her left but I barely notice that. While trying to figure out how I can smell Lily so clearly when she is so far away, I stare at the woman to Kathy's left.

She seems like she's in her late twenties. She's looking ahead with a bemused smile on her face, only half-listening to Kathy's chatter. Long blonde hair frames her stunning face. She is taller than Lily but she wears stylish open-toed heeled shoes. Her jeans cling to her legs the way every girl wishes Calvin Klein would. She's wearing a V-necked thick white T-shirt that fits loosely over her large breasts.

"Pete," I whisper urgently. This was a five-alarm alert and I think he's still looking the wrong way.

He isn't. I glance towards him and see that his radar has already gone off, pointing him in the right direction.

I look back. Kathy and Lily see us and smile. Lily's sweet scent somehow crosses the distance but I push it aside. The woman near Lily is looking at me, too, her full red lips still half-pulled up in a small smile.

That steamy warmth washes over me again.

I gasp and it burns my lungs. The heat. It's coming from her.

What's going on?

There's no time to think about it.

I take a couple of tentative steps forward and Pete moves up beside me.

"Hey," he says, as the girls come to a stop in front of us.

Thank God Pete says something because I can't. Between that humid heat coming off the goddess beside Kathy and the amazing musk of Lily herself, I can barely breathe. I'm blinking rapidly, trying to focus on what's happening, how it can be happening.

Kathy glances at me, grinning awkwardly. I know her well enough to realize she wasn't expecting Pete to be here with me. She smoothes her hair quickly with one hand and looks at him with a steady, even smile.

"Hello, Pete," Lily says, her eyes already moving to my face. "Hi, Sam," she says, her voice higher and brighter.

"This is my mom. Cindy, these are my friends Sam and Pete."

The perfect woman, now known as Cindy, holds out her manicured hand to me.

How the hell can this beauty queen be Lily's mom? Big sister, definitely, but mom?

My manners take over, derailing the freight train of confusion in my head. I grab her hand and shake it quickly. She has a good grip and our eyes meet. They are bright blue and shiny.

"Hi, Sam."

"Hi, Cindy," I say, my voice sounding flat and distant. She holds my hand for an extra second and stares at me intently. There is a question in her eyes now but it passes quickly and she lets go. My hand falls back to my side, feeling like I just plunged it into a hot tub to test how warm the water was.

Cindy now turns to Pete. Unlike me, Pete knows what to do and what to say around women.

He clutches her hand and turns up that full grin and warm eyes of his.

"Hi, Cindy. I'm Pete Gibbons. It's great to meet you."

Cindy's hand lingers in Pete's longer than it had in mine but there is no uncertainty.

"Hi, Pete," she smiles broadly. "I've heard you've been very nice to Lily at school."

"Oh, yeah," Pete's right hand is now smacking my shoulder. He's putting on a charm school. "Not as nice as Sam but I do what I can."

"That's true," Lily says, moving to stand beside me and face Cindy and Kathy. Lily's hand grabs my arm gently. "Sam has been so sweet to me. He walks me to

35

school every day."

"You guys only live a block away," I say through the thick wool sock stuffed in my mouth. I lick my bottom lip nervously and look at Cindy.

"Well, I should go," Cindy says, glancing at her watch, her hair shimmering around her head. "I have some clients to see this afternoon."

She looks at Lily. "I won't be in until late, okay?"

Before Lily can answer, Cindy's eyes move to me.

"It was good to meet you, Sam." The same questioning look is in her eyes, like she has met me before but can't remember where. "I'm sure I'll be seeing more of you soon."

I nod.

"Kathy," she says, raising her left hand to Kathy's elbow and smiling.

Then, before dropping her hand from Kathy, she takes a half-step forward and brushes her fingers slightly on Pete's left arm.

"Pete," she says in passing.

"I'll see you both later."

She is already moving past us towards the doors.

Everyone except me says bye to Cindy at the same time.

Lily squeezes my arm and I choke out a quiet bye, too.

What just happened?

In a smooth and natural way, Cindy touched Kathy and Pete at the same time, for just an instant. In that half-second, I felt an electrical charge go through the air, like a welder forged a link between two sheets of metal. The air's now thick and wet from a lightning storm. Neither Kathy nor Pete seems to notice. What has Cindy done? She has changed something between Kathy and Pete.

Cindy touched them, together, and now everything is different.

Nobody says anything for a second as we watch Cindy reach the doors. Two guys, one about my dad's age, the other even older, are practically tripping over each other to hold the door for her.

"That's your MOM?" Kathy breaks the silence. "Jeez, I wish I had puppies like that."

I smirk and glance at Lily. Kathy has a directness I've always liked so that's not what's different now.

"You and me both," Lily agrees, nodding her head.

"Like you guys didn't notice," Kathy gives Pete a playful elbow in the ribs.

"Well…" Pete says, shrugging. A rare moment. Pete speechless.

The poke just now by Kathy, the physical contact with Pete, who suddenly can't talk. Something is definitely happening here but I still can't figure out what it is. I realize it's my turn to talk.

"I thought she was hot," I say.

Kathy giggles. Lily glances at me with a curious expression but says nothing.

"So, how can we be of service to you two attractive young ladies?" Pete says, trying to change the topic and regain control of the situation.

"Take us where we want to go and don't complain," Kathy says, wrapping her hands around one of Pete's arms and leaning into him.

Hmm. Kathy is never this forward with Pete. She always plays it cool with him, hanging back. Because of that, I don't think Pete ever notices her. Not that way, anyway. Now he's walking with her, talking, focusing on her, in a way I haven't seen him do ever before, like he honestly cares what she's saying and thinking. Did Cindy somehow make this happen when she touched them? And if she did, how?

Lily lets Kathy guide us around the mall. The girls scoot into a clothing store, circling around the racks like hummingbirds. Pete stays surprisingly close to Kathy, smiling constantly, offering feedback. I stand back a little further and say nothing. Lily catches my eye from time to time and smiles. I smile back, confused.

At the third store, when the girls finally find something to try on and duck into a change room, I turn to Pete.

"What are you doing?"

"Shopping with the girls, buddy," he says, looking at me suspiciously.

"No, no, no…" I keep my voice down. I can hear the girls behind the doors, wrestling into their new jeans.

"When did you suddenly get hot for Kathy?" I ask, more coldly than I intended. Knowing her feelings for Pete, I have to admit I'm protective of her. I don't want her to be hurt because Pete is practicing or, worse yet, showing off when his real target is Lily.

"Easy, man. It's cool. I know you and Kathy are tight. I just kinda realized how awesome she is. She's not all girly around me, she's just herself. I like that." He's staring at Kathy's change room door with a distant expression on his face.

"So what about the yummy new girl?" I ask.

Pete looks at me.

"Just keeping the road clear for you, chum," he says with a fake smile, looking back to the change rooms. The girls are coming out, admiring themselves in the mirrors.

"Yeah, sure," I reply. Something's still not right.

We wander around the mall for a couple of hours. The

girls buy a few things and Pete carries the bags. Kathy is glowing with all the attention from both Pete and Lily. I look just interested enough and speak just often enough that they never ask me if I'm bored.

We hit the food court for an early dinner, eating and people watching.

"So what does your mom do, Lily?" Kathy asks around a mouthful of fried rice.

"She's a midwife. She delivers babies," Lily answers between sips of lemonade.

"Like a doctor?" Pete cuts in.

"No, no," Lily replies. "Midwives just work with pregnant women. Well, sometimes she offers help to women trying to get pregnant but usually she just helps with the pregnancy and the delivery."

"And your dad?" Kathy asks.

"There's no dad," Lily says, picking up her sub. "Just me and Cindy."

"My mom's a single mom, too," Pete says. "But I have two sisters."

"That explains why you're so good with the girls," Lily laughs.

"Don't forget his amazing good looks," I chime in.

Pete acts wounded and Kathy pats him on the shoulder, telling him in a soothing voice that we aren't very nice and to ignore the mean people.

Later on, we leave the mall and walk across Cooper to the theatres. The girls sit together with Pete on one side, next to Kathy, and me on the other with Lily. We share popcorn and watch a comedy about two guys out of college who open a coffee shop called Fresh Pot Brewing as a front for selling dope out the back door. They're getting lots of business, even from cops, politicians and the parents of kids they went to high school with, but then some gang guys show up, looking for their cut.

Halfway through the show, I glance over and notice Pete has his arm on the armrest next to Kathy. She has her hand on his arm. They look happy.

After, we share our favourite moments from the movie as we head outside. It's nearly dark and the air has cooled. We walk back to my mom's van and pile inside. The girls sit together in the back and Pete climbs in the front passenger seat.

"Where to?"

"Home for me, man," Pete says, grumpily.

"What?" I key the engine.

"Yeah, the only way I could get cash out of my mom was to babysit my niece and nephew tonight. They're sleeping over at our house."

"Well, who's looking after them now?" I ask, pulling out of our parking stall.

"Your sister. You'll be picking her up when you drop me off."

The girls start teasing Pete about his upcoming babysitting chores while I drive to his house. They are still on him pretty good ("Why don't you open a daycare after graduation?" "Maybe my mom could refer you to her pregnant ladies." "Oh, I bet he's great with diapers." "Sing us a Barney song, Pete.") when we get to his house on St. Amand Road.

"Thanks for the great time, ladies," he says, sarcastically, opening the door. "Anytime you need babysitting, I'm a phone call away. I'll send Sara out."

"Yeah, sure," I say. "Later."

Pete shuts the door and runs to the front step.

The girls start making plans for some school event

next week. Pete's at the front door giving Sara some excuse to hurry up and get out of his house. I chuckle quietly. She waves to him and walks over to the van.

"Hey, Sara," I say. "This is our friend Lily." I motion to the back seat.

"Hi," she says, not even bothering to glance back at Lily. Instead, Sara just sits there as stiff and stupid as usual.

"Hey, Sara," both girls reply.

"How's Grade 7 going? Do you have Mr. Johnson this year?" Kathy asks.

"Not good," Sara answers, turning the radio on. "Mr. Johnson is an old dork."

Kathy and I laugh. Sara sits with her arms crossed, looking out into the night as I drive Kathy over to her place on Richter. Kathy's explaining to Lily why every kid who's ever had Mr. Johnson thinks he's an old dork. She tells the story about how June is unbearable in his class because the school doesn't have air conditioning and Mr. Johnson sweats through his shirt long before lunch. By the time the final bell rings, his class is choking on old man B.O. Pete anonymously got him some antiperspirant for Christmas the year we had him but it didn't seem to register.

By the time Kathy is done with her story, I'm pulling up in front of her townhouse.

"I had a great time, guys. Let's do it again," she says cheerfully, sliding the door open and grabbing her bag from shopping.

"Call me tomorrow," Lily answers.

"Okay." Kathy shuts the door and waves as I drive the van away.

Nobody speaks as I drive the few short blocks to the

house. I tap the steering wheel with my fingers in time to the music on the radio.

"Aren't you bringing Lily home?" Sara asks as I turn into our driveway and hit the garage door opener.

"Nah, I'll walk her home. She just lives on the next block," I answer nonchalantly.

Sara is out of the van before I even shut it off. She's inside the house by the time Lily and I finish getting out. Lily grabs her bag and I shut the sliding door for her. I hit the garage door remote again, slam the van's door shut and we dash out as the garage door slides down behind us.

"Did you have fun?" I ask as we turn on the sidewalk and head towards Lily's house.

"That was great," she replies. "I didn't think I'd make friends so fast. Everyone's so nice."

"Well, it's kinda you, too."

"Thanks, Sam," she purrs, moving closer to me. "You know, Pete's not the only one who knows how to charm a girl. You have your ways, too."

I blow out a short sharp breath of disbelief. "Yeah, sure."

"No, really. I've talked about you all the time this week, according to my mom. Speaking of her, I think you made quite an impression."

"What? With your mom? All we did was say hi."

"You don't know her."

"What are you talking about? Was I that bad?"

There's a laugh in her answer.

"Oh, no. You were fine. Really."

"That's it?"

"What did you think of my mom?" she asks abruptly.

We walk in silence for a moment. A car goes by. The night is clear and calm. Despite Lily's stated confidence in my so-called charm, I'm getting more nervous with each step we get closer to her house. I don't want our night together to end yet. I feel drawn to Lily. It isn't that protective urge I feel with Kathy, like I need to be the one guarding her from all the jerks of the world. It's something more magnetic that seems to come from deeper inside. I want her and her scent and her soft fingers all to myself.

"Your turn," she says, softly cutting into my thoughts. "You said she was hot."

I take a deep breath of the night air. Its coolness is a nice accompaniment to Lily's rich smell, which seems to swirl gently around us. The stars are out over the mountains to the west and south.

"Okay," I say, my voice too loud in my ears. "I'll tell you what I think about your mom but you have to walk with me down to the lake tonight and you have to promise not to laugh."

"Absolutely, Sam."

I look over. There is no laugh, only her smiling face.

"Let me drop my bag inside the house. Then take me to the lake and tell me how hot she is."

She sprints ahead to her front door, cutting across three front lawns on the way, her bag banging against her leg. By the time I walk up the sidewalk, she has already locked her front door again and is jogging back to me.

Great. I want to tell this girl I'm crazy for her. First I have to tell her that her mom is a walking wet dream. Should I mention the steamy heat I felt from a hundred feet away or should I just mention the big boobs? And what about that little trick she did with Pete and Sara?

Still haven't figured that out yet.

Even when we squeezed our eyes shut
Screaming
To hide
The faces of the angels shone in our minds
Bright and calm and staring
And just and knowing
It hurt even more
When we remembered
They hated us.

Diving (Lily)

I pause inside the dark house for a second before running back to him.

How is this possible?

He senses us from a distance yet his mind is intact.

He felt Cindy solidify the link between Pete and Kathy.

His grip on his sanity should be slipping yet the opposite is happening.

He is increasingly lucid in his awareness.

I want him so bad.

He is perfect.

He sees me.

He wants to be with me and I want him to know everything about me.

I want to tell him that I am Lilith, the first wife of Adam (and Cindy, the Eve, is the second). I want him to know that I am The Raven. I am the Dark Moon. Cindy and I together are the Three Witches. I am Freya. I am Radha. I am Shiva. I am Guanyin. I am Isis. I am Neith. I am the Virgin and Cindy is the Whore of Babylon. I am Athena. Cindy is Aphrodite. I am all the prayers offered and all the sacrifices made.

Cindy is their miracles.

In her human form, Cindy is a 30-year-old woman who revels in the creation of the new.

Cindy is carnal knowledge. She is the consummation, the moment the sperm unites with the egg, the seed bursting forth into the soil. She is the creator of humanity. It was she who gave them their shape. She saw to it that they made themselves in our image.

He felt what she represents today but he does not know what it means.

He is so innocent and pure.

I want Cindy to erase all of my names and all of my past. I want her to make me human and forge Sam and me together, just like she did for Pete and Kathy.

I should be more cautious but my desire is overwhelming me.

I am vulnerable.

I am running back to him.

Knowing (Amara)

He holds out a hand to me as he approaches.

He speaks.

"Come, Amara. Let us walk."

I take his hand.

He guides me to the door and I do not hesitate before it.

When the sunlight hits my face, I stop, turning my face towards it, staring into its bright beauty. I can see again.

"Thank you, Bodie."

He lets go of my hand.

"Listen to what I have to say about your creation before you thank me. You would not listen before but you must hear me now."

I feel my face tugging upwards from the sides. My lips part and I show him my teeth. I am smiling.

"Of course, Bodie. Of course. You are correct."

Diving (Sam)

"Was it just me or was your sister rude to me?" Lily asks as she reaches my side. We turn up the block.

I still have Cindy on the brain but it's easy to switch gears and crap all over my little sister for a while. Sara and I have always had an awkward relationship. Mom and Dad expected me to be big brother to her from the moment they brought her home but I resented having to share my parents with her. I guess that's what comes with being five years old and old enough to remember when this intruder comes into your house.

Not just any intruder. All she did was cry for the first three months for hours on end, starting just after dinner. I never understood the thing about the cute baby because that little face of hers would get all red and the only thing that came out of her mouth was air-raid siren. I remember one of my only spankings from Dad was after two hours of it one night; I came out of my room in my pajamas with my pillow in my hand and offered to hold the pillow over her face until Sara stopped that endless crying.

I didn't know what that meant. I just wanted to help. With Sara still wailing in his arm, Dad jumped to his feet, his face all cloudy with fury, spun me around and gave me three really hard swats on my butt. He didn't say a word. He dragged me by the arm down the hall, pushed me into my room towards my bed and slammed the door.

I buried my face in my pillow, my tears burning. I tried to hold my head in there until I got away from Sara's crying, which seemed to be worse than ever.

That was our good start and it didn't get much better after that.

"It wasn't her fault," Lily cuts in as we wait at the corner for a car to go by so we can cross and head up Rose Avenue towards the lakeshore. "She was a colicky baby."

"Colicky? What's that?"

"It's a word I learned from my mom. Some babies get this thing called colic. They just cry for hours at a time for no reason and you can't do anything to comfort them. Nobody's really sure why it happens but it stops after they're a few months old."

"Really? I thought all babies did that."

"Does that change your memories of Sara as a baby?"

"God, no."

"I'm curious about her," Lily says, slowly.

"Well, that makes one of us," I answer.

I start telling Lily other stories from my childhood. Sara's toys, especially her dolls, became the subjects of endless experiments that usually involved their destruction. Throwing one in the oven when Mom was baking a cake (spanking). I plugged up the toilet once by trying to flush some. Two of them actually went down and Dad had to call a plumber (another spanking). When I was 10, I ran over one of her Barbies with the lawnmower. Another time, I think I was 11 or 12, I got Dad's hatchet out of the shed, cut up one of her favorite dolls into five or six pieces and then glued them back together in a different order, so the head was where the stomach should have been and the feet were on top and the hands on the bottom.

"She had nightmares from that one for weeks," I chuckle.

"You're telling me all this to show what a sensitive guy you are?" Lily asks.

Nice move, Cassanova. Tell your poorly adjusted, how-I-became-a-serial-killer stories to the girl you'd like to hook up with.

I get all defensive, blaming Mom and Dad for spending so much time with her and dropping me like cat litter, blaming Sara for being so demanding and milking all the attention.

"And it's your fault, too," I blurt at her. "You get me all relaxed and then I start blabbing and telling you all these stupid stories about torturing my baby sister and being a jerk."

I glance over and catch Lily's face from the lights across the street. Her eyes crinkle and her nose bunches up as she holds her lips together, sucking in short little breaths through her nose so she won't laugh.

There's no traffic at Water Street as we cross into Strathcona Park. The lights from the homes on the west side, across the lake, glitter on the water. We can already hear small waves lapping against the shore as we walk across the grass and then the sand towards the dark water.

"You aren't a jerk, Sam," she says in a tender voice. "You were just a boy, thinking boy ways and doing boy things."

"We're still not close or anything. That's why she ignored you. Any girl that would want to hang out with me must be a loser. She can't help but like Kathy, though."

"Kathy is wonderful, isn't she?"

Lily slips her shoes off. She isn't wearing any socks so she just walks right into the water up to her ankles.

I'm wearing these old sandals so I walk in with her, the coolness of the water calming me as I start telling some Kathy stories.

There's a small spectator, standing in the back of the stands of my brain and I can hear him. Stop talking. Stop telling all these stupid childhood stories. Stop boring her to tears. Can't you think of anything else to talk about? Do you like to hear yourself talk? Do you think she'd like to get a word in? Stop talking. Stop talking.

Over his protests, I tell Lily all about Kathy. How we met when she moved to town in Grade 2. How our moms became best friends because they both volunteered at our school. How our dads started going snowmobiling together on weekends in the winter. How Sara became best friends forever with Kathy's younger sister Melanie.

And I remembered the time I got sent to the principal's office in Grade 3 for punching Kevin Dempster in the face, giving him a bleeding nose, after he pushed Kathy into a mud puddle and she scraped her hand and got her clothes all wet and dirty. She didn't cry. She got up slowly, looking at her hand so I made sure Kevin Dempster did some crying. As he stood there, yelling and holding his face and the blood started running between his fingers, Kathy ran over and started screaming at Kevin.

He was a bully, he was stupid, she hoped he liked getting hit in the face, she asked him how it would feel to pick his nose in class now and she hoped it was broken and he would grow up with an ugly crooked nose like a witch and everyone would stay away from the ugly boy with the ugly nose on an ugly face.

She was still shouting at him when Mrs. Walters ran over.

I don't remember what the principal said.

I just remember my dad sitting on my bed that night and patting me on the arm as I lay under the sheets, waiting for him to scold me like Mom had at the supper table. He called me son and he never did that. And he said I did the right thing and he was proud of me for standing up for a girl against a bully.

Kathy and I have been best of friends from then on.

"So that's why you're not so keen on Pete and Kathy getting together?"

I look at her, startled.

She stares back at me. Had Lily felt what I had felt when Cindy touched them? Or had she just noticed all the flirting in the mall and at the movie? How could she not?

I sigh.

"They're my two best friends. I don't think I could ever talk to him again if he hurt her and Pete and me have been friends since we were little. Pete's my friend but I don't like the way he talks about girls sometimes. He can be mean. He knows he's smarter than most people so he puts them down and a lot of times he doesn't even know he's doing it. And he goes through girlfriends like nothing. Six weeks, two months, he's bored."

"You sound jealous, Sam."

"No. Well, maybe. Ok, yeah, sure. I'm the nerdy friend of the cool jock guy. But I still worry if something happens between him and Kathy."

"Oh, I think they're past ifs."

"Really?"

"You didn't notice that Kathy didn't mind being brought home right away? If they aren't texting, they're already talking on the phone."

"If Kathy's on the phone, she'll never hang up."

"Says the guy who has been talking the whole time

here."

"Sorry."

"No, that's great. I like how you're comfortable around me. I don't get that a lot."

"What do you mean? Half the school knows who you are already and you just started there."

"I do great with first impressions but I have trouble after that. It doesn't take long around me and people start thinking of things they would rather be doing and people they'd rather be hanging around with."

"That's crap."

Lily steps back out of the water, bends to pick up her shoes in one hand and turns to walk up the beach. I follow, my wet sandals sticking to the sand.

"Sam, you've only known me for five days," she says quietly. There's disappointment and sadness in her voice. "You don't know my life."

"Sorry. You're right. I don't know what I'm talking about."

The spectator in the stands in my head is now jumping up and down, yelling at the clown on the field who is me. Don't do it. Don't you dare. Don't you even try it. You are an idiot.

I ignore him again. It's time to throw a pass down field.

"I do know what I think about you. You made a great first impression and the more I see you, the more I like you."

The spectator covers his face with his hands. The crowd holds its breath.

As natural as I can, I drift my right hand into her left hand beside me.

She grabs it and doesn't let go.

I feel her scent again, sighing, pleased. It's like it reflects what she's feeling. It makes me feel so good to know I've done the right thing and she's cool with it. I don't know how I know, just through that perfume, but I'm as sure of it as I am my own name.

"Thanks, Sam. That makes me happy for you to say that."

"How could I not like you?" I breathe. "That perfume makes me a little crazy."

Lily turns to face me, pulling me to a stop. She's about four inches shorter than me so her eyes are close. They're grabbing all the bits of surrounding light and reflecting them in a concentrated burst back at me.

"How crazy?"

She's looking at me more seriously than I expect, like she wants an honest answer, not just another compliment. Without thinking, I just tell her the truth.

"I can smell you in my dreams. I know when you're coming when you're still far away. It lets me know you're happy. It makes me feel calm and safe and say things that I know don't make sense but they make sense to me."

Without breaking her gaze, she steps closer, until our bodies are almost touching. She takes my other hand.

"I won't laugh at you, Sam."

My lungs stop working. My heart explodes. I can't see the crowd in my head anymore. It's too bright. All I can see now are her dark eyes, her delicate smile.

"But enough about me," she chuckles, stepping back, breaking the moment with the soft tinkling of bells from the back of her throat. "You're still on the hook to tell me how hot my mom is."

"Right. Well, she's got—"

"I know, I know, the boobs, the hair, blahblahblahblah. I know all about my mom."

We start walking again. Without asking each other, we slowly head across the grass and out of the park, in the direction of home.

"What's she like, I mean, as a mom?" I ask.

Lily falls silent. She's somewhere else and I don't push. There's a chill in the air now and we walk back much quicker than we had walked to the lake. When we're a block away, I decide to break Lily's thoughts up.

"You know, I heard you call her a slut."

"What?" she laughs. "When?" She doesn't sound like she believes me.

"The first day of school, when we first met. I was coming up the sidewalk and you came to the door and said—"

"Cindy, you are such a slut. Right, I remember."

She's quiet again and stays that way until we stop in front of her house.

"Can I tell you about my mom another time? Our relationship is, well, we get along great but it's…well, it's different."

"Complicated," I offer.

"Yeah," she breathes, looking down the street, but not seeing the street. "Complicated. That's a good word."

"Are you okay?"

She looks at me with an intensity that takes me by surprise. She steps close again, staring into my face. Our eyes meet. She puts her free hand on my shoulder.

Suddenly, I'm scared. She wants to tell me something, something important. The air feels cold on my bare arm. The real boyfriend in Vancouver? Let's just be friends? Cindy won't approve? I'm going to the convent to be a nun? What? The answer isn't what I expect.

"With you, Sam, I always feel okay," she says, smiling quietly. As she speaks, I can feel her scent again, pushing deep into my senses, confirming what she's saying. I relax.

Her face moves closer. That sweet musk seems to be coming from her every pore, from her breath as she whispers in that same lower tone she used when she had seen my notebook.

"You perceive me at a deeper level, Sam. I have to consider whether I am attracted to your perception of me or to you as a person. Maybe it is both. You should be dangerous to me, a threat, but I do not feel it when I am with you. I feel safe in your presence. I feel like I want to protect you. I am not afraid but you must be patient with me. These are new feelings for me. Will you give me some time?"

"Yeah, yeah, sure, of course," I can barely breathe. The hairs on my neck and arms are vibrating, electric.

"Okay," she smiles, herself again. She steps back and squeezes my hand before letting it go.

Through the open front window in her house, I can hear the phone ringing.

She jams her hand into her pocket and yanks her keys out.

"I have to go. That'll be Kathy, I think. I bet she wants to tell me all about Pete."

She's walking backwards up the sidewalk to the front step.

"I'll call you tomorrow. Bye."

She turns, pushes the key into the door and is inside in a second. A light comes on and she catches the phone on the fourth ring. Her voice is too quiet for me to hear. A car goes by, waking me up. My feet turn towards home, dragging my brain behind.

What just happened? We're together but she wants to go slow, I think. We would have to talk about her using that serious voice on me. That's twice now that she starts talking like she's a different person, speaking all formal and strange. How could I be dangerous? What deeper level was she talking about?

Well, she sees me as a person, so that's a start, I think, smiling to myself.

Our tears burned the lacerations across our
  face
We couldn't stop staring
They were so beautiful
So magnificent
So above us
So deadly
We just wanted to die to worship them
They were here to save us
And obliterate our existence from history
We all wanted to be the first.

Ending (Amara)

"Bodie, what will happen to me?"

We are sitting on the sand. He is looking out across the water, his legs stretched out in front of him with his arms behind him. I am cross-legged, facing him.

He still does not look at me but concentrates on the waves lapping at the shore.

"You mean when you die?"

I look down at my bare toes. Sand has crept in between them.

That word makes me uncomfortable and he knows it.

"You can call it what you want, Amara. The ending. The dark. It makes no difference to me."

"Yes, when I die," I mutter softly.

He turns to me and smiles.

"She will take you away from all of this."

His voice is gentle.

"That's all? Where will I be? Will I be with Samael? Will I find our creator?" I ask, my voice rising.

I stop and take a deep breath, closing my eyes. I must control myself. I have not worked so hard and for so long to betray my intentions now. Lilith will feel me, will know my desires and she will find me here if I am not cautious. I cannot face her yet.

Bodie is kneeling in front of me now, his arms around my body, pulling me gently into him. My face rests against his shirt, which smells dusty.

I feel his words vibrate through his chest and into my head.

"I approached her once a long time ago, when she let herself have a physical form. She had the appearance of a young human girl. To speak to me, I had to take her hand. She is the doorway to a place I do not know. I am fascinated by what lies beyond her and I think about her constantly but I am not ready to die yet. Maybe you will be with Samael again and all your questions will have answers but I do not believe so."

"What do you believe?" I whisper into his shirt.

He laughs and pulls away from me. The bristles on the side of his face scratch my skin as his lips stop just before my ear.

"Nothing," he breathes. "But I know what you believe.

You are right about Sam but not in the way you think."

"What do you mean? Have we made a mistake with Samael?" I ask as he stands up.

He is walking away, towards the water but his voice carries back to me.

"We have accomplished what no other guardian, not even Cindy, has ever done. We have created another living being like us, with my knowing and your spark of light, and he is what we made of him but he is more than a mere guardian. He is human."

What a perfect thing to say.

I cannot keep my happiness inside. I sigh and smile, turning my face to the sun again.

The weather is so beautiful.

The days are almost done.

The stars are brightly shining (Sam)

As the leaves turn bright and fall, the last of the fruit is harvested in the orchards, and the sky, the lake and the mountainsides all turn grey, the dreams change with the season.

I still can't see her in my dreams but I don't need to. I can just draw that scent into myself and she's there, laughing, eyes shining. I can hear the people more, too. I can take a breath and know their whole story.

At a traffic light, there's a trucker who wants to switch satellite radio providers, wants a good meal, hot coffee and a decent night's sleep that would last a week. Wants his boss to fall under the tires of his rig, accidentally on purpose.

On the curb waiting to cross the street is a lady in business suit who wants the repair bill on the van to be not too much. She wants to lose weight but wants a milkshake, a big vanilla one, and a cheeseburger.

Next to her is an old lady who wants her priest to say something more meaningful than 'open your heart to God, Agnes.' Wants her kids to go to church and visit more often and her grandchildren to behave better and stop playing video games and swearing.

And then, sometimes, entwined in the Lily scent, I can feel Cindy's heat. The trucker wants his wife to hurt him and call him terrible names. He wants to beg her to stop and he wants her not to. The old lady wants a man half her age to touch her and feel her.

And then their desires spin out of control. They want everything so much and so soon that I can feel their minds slipping away from them, their greed eating their brains like a cancer. Lily's smell becomes overwhelming, a sour and rotting stench that makes me gag, while that humid warmth of Cindy's only enhances that feeling of something once alive now in full decomposition, wet and foul.

I always wake up with Lily's scent in the room, the walls too close, the sheets kicked off. Sometimes it feel like Cindy's heat is there too and I find myself burning with sweat and aroused. My head always pounds, like there's too much being stuffed into it.

So I get up and try to write, but the words seem false, like I'm not following the recipe right, missing something urgent.

Mom knocks on the door at about 4 a.m. as I'm working.

"Sam?" She knocks and opens the door at the same time. What's the point of a door if they aren't willing to wait until you say 'come in' before they just march right inside? The little knock and the concerned voice somehow make it ok.

"Yes, Mom?" I say, impatiently, not looking up from the papers scattered on my desk.

"What are you doing? Your father said he saw your light on."

"So he woke you up to come and ask me?" I ask with a flat, cool voice, turning to look at her. It's less a question than an accusation.

Mom glances at the rumpled sheets on my bed and then out the window. I let her dwell on the possibility that there has been someone in the room with me who has made a sudden escape. My room is on the ground floor with the window easily accessible from the backyard.

In the meantime, I'm thinking about Dad getting up to use the john because he can't make it through the night without a tinkle break. He sees the light on underneath the door and stands in the hallway, his bare feet getting chilly on the laminate floor, unsure what to do. Finally, the logical thing pops into his mind—wake up the boy's mother and send her in. He's probably already sleeping again.

"Is it homework?" she says, ignoring my question and giving me a way out.

"Yeah, Mom. Couldn't sleep."

Her face brightens. She can sleep now and she knows the answer will get a grunt of approval from Dad over their morning coffee, a few hours from now. By then, I'll be trying to grab some last minutes of rest before getting up, showering and racing off to pick up Lily for school.

I keep meaning to ask Lily about her scent and my dreams but there's never a right time and it just seems stupid. How do you casually ask "Hey, I can smell you from a distance, not that that's a bad thing, and you're in my dreams every night. Do you know anything about that?" Anyhow, all of the worry falls away whenever she smiles at me.

The next few months with Lily aren't like my six weeks with Paula last year. Going out with Paula was intense every minute of every day. We were the first for each other so it was all new, all the time. We spent so much time loving the moments together that we forgot about the other person. It was the experience we were enjoying, not each other.

And then the novelty wore off and suddenly the annoying familiarity took over. Those little quirks everyone has became painful itches we couldn't scratch. She was hot for me but hated the sound of me chewing gum. I was crazy to be with her but hated that high little gasp she tacked on to the end of her laugh. Her lipstick was amazing but why did she have to put so much on that it got on my clothes when she kissed my neck?

We went from being obsessed with each other, where we couldn't stand being apart, and if we were, we were talking on the phone or texting, to being obsessed with trying to make each other more what we had in mind. In the end, we couldn't even agree on how to break up. I wanted to keep working to fix it; she just wanted to get away from me before I drove her totally crazy.

She was a grade behind me so it was easy to ignore each other, even in a school as small as K.L.O.

As fall becomes early winter and Christmas holidays approach, Lily and I settle into this quiet togetherness. We hold hands walking to and from school but rarely spend time together at school because of her busy schedule.

On weeknights, we go for walks after dinner, stopping in at a coffee place for a drink and to warm up. Before I met her, I couldn't stand the bitterness of coffee, now I drink it hot and black, the heat and the sharpness and the rich nuttiness underneath, filling me with warmth. I feel like I am changing.

We talk but never in a rush. Sometimes we don't speak at all, watching our breath in the chilly night air as we walk, listening to the pull and push of the air in our lungs or watching the other customers in the coffee shop. Our conversations always seem hushed, like we just want to share the sound of our voices with only each other. We laugh a lot because we're rarely serious. I think her laugh is perfect—it starts at the bottom of her toes and percolates out of her mouth in these tiny little bubbles that float across the air.

We don't kiss until nearly Halloween, more than six weeks after that first walk by the lake. Even the kiss is a bit of an accident, unplanned, unrushed. She is over at my house on a Sunday afternoon and we're doing our homework together at the kitchen table. Needing a break, she's getting some juice out of the fridge and I'm pulling down some glasses from the cupboard. A ceramic coffee mug falls out and drops to the floor, smashing into about four or five chunks and quite a few smaller pieces.

She kneels down and picks them up while I grab a little hand broom from under the sink and sweep up the rest, muttering to myself. We stand up together. I hold out the pan and she drops the bigger pieces into it.

"It's just one of Dad's old mugs, he's got a billion of them," I say as I dump the fragments in the garbage and put the broom and pan away.

When I stand straight again to face her, she's right there, her right hand coming to rest on my hip, the other hand reaching out to touch my cheek. She's smiling.

"It's an ancient tradition for the man to break a cup.

It means we live in an imperfect world, where things can be broken, but it will be as difficult to separate us as it would be to reunite those broken pieces."

"What are you—?"

Before I can finish asking how we went from a broken green coffee mug that says John Deere Tractor on the side in yellow to fussy old romantic traditions I've never heard of, her mouth is against my lips.

She doesn't wear lipstick (or makeup at all as far as I can tell) but the taste of her lips reminds me of the cinnamon on the top of apple pie. Her soothing scent washes over me, coming from her skin and her breath as she gasps, her lips apart, pushing the air that had been in her lungs, past her teeth and lips, into my startled mouth, onto my tongue.

I keep my eyes closed, even after she pulls her mouth away.

"Mmm…," I start, my voice heavy and deep. "You were saying something about ancient traditions."

She slaps my arm and I open my eyes to her. She's still standing close and her other hand is still on my cheek.

"Let's get that juice and finish our homework. Maybe we'll talk some more about ancient traditions later."

"Yeah, sure."

She pulls away, chuckling softly.

The kisses become daily things but they never last long—a few seconds when I pick her up in the morning or walking her back to her house in the cold night. They are simple and calm and relaxed as all of our time together, like we have the rest of eternity. There's no rush. Time has stopped for us, yet it speeds up all around us.

We hang out with Pete and Kathy sometimes but there isn't much room in their togetherness for distraction. As calm as Lily and I are together, Pete and Kathy's relationship is this desperate panic, like they are trying to make up for lost time. They can't keep their hands or their minds off each other.

They change. Pete looks even broader at the shoulders, stronger, more masculine if that's possible. He still harasses me whenever he sees me, the only time when Kathy scolds him, but it's less harsh, more respectful. Kathy acquires a glow. Her red hair and her round face and blue eyes just seem to get brighter as the days grow darker. She walks with a confidence I don't remember her having before, like she knows where she's going and how she's getting there and her future is certain.

When Pete is away for a few days, for a volleyball tournament in Vancouver or Kamloops, Kathy mopes around like a zombie, her body present but her eyes somewhere else. Lily and I take her with us to the mall or a movie and even for a walk and a coffee. She seems to pick up with the two of us there, chatty and energetic with Lily, her familiar sister-like self with me.

"How are you and Lily?" she asks one Saturday night in late November, as we stand by the statue of the white sails at the end of Bernard Avenue, waiting for Lily. Pete's away at the provincial championships in Vancouver. The downtown businesses are having their Christmas lights celebration. All the storefronts are decorated with lights and traditional displays of holiday cheer in their windows. There are people everywhere, sipping hot drinks, listening to the choirs sing their familiar carols. The street is closed to traffic, except for a few wagons on wheels, drawn by horses, families sitting together on hay bales in the back. We're going to walk around and then head over to the old memorial arena to go skating.

"Nice," I say, not looking at Kathy but scanning the crowd for Lily. It's only that Christmas is here that I realize Lily feels like Christmas—warm in the surrounding cold, a scent of spice and cider and chocolate and pine. I can feel her all around me.

"It's good to see you with her," she says. She moves up next to me and hooks an arm around one of my arms. "You two seem so…so easy with each other. It seems like you're connected even when you're not together. God, with Pete, I need to be touching him all the time when we're together and when we're alone, I just want to smother him and—"

"Thanks for the picture, Kathy. I think I get it," I say, more grumpily than I really mean. I'm happy for them but I rarely look at them when they are together. When they're apart, I can take it, I know who they are, but together, it's hard. It's like they've mutated into something I don't recognize, something a little too hot and bright for me to look at. I can feel their need so bad that I feel I'm intruding.

"Sorry," she says, squeezing my arm. "I'm sorry I'm turning into one of those annoying bitches who ask how her friends are only as an excuse so she can talk about herself. I just wanted to know how you are doing. You know, how you are really doing."

"I'm good, pumpkin," I say, using her old pet name from our elementary school days. I look over at her face and pat her arm. "Better than ever."

"You look tired at school," she blurts. "And there's something with Lily, too. She's nervous about something. She's holding back."

"What do you mean?" I reply, turning quickly to Kathy. I can't see Lily yet but I know she will be here in a minute or two. And that sudden rush of warmth, like it's not a month from Christmas in Kelowna but July in Miami. Cindy is with her.

Kathy's girl instincts flip a switch in my head. Kathy's right. I've been so preoccupied with being with Lily that I haven't taken a step back. I still don't understand how or why I can feel Lily so much. Like now, so close, and Cindy, too. That's not right. And I know what Kathy means. Lily had said so herself, that night we first went to the beach, in that voice of hers, which wasn't her normal voice but something else. What is she holding back?

"I think Lily's great, Sam, and I think she's great for you, but…"

There they are. Lily's bouncing down the sidewalk like her feet are barely touching the fancy red bricks, her face all lit up, taking in all the holiday atmosphere like she's a little kid and this is her first Christmas. Cindy looks bored, her hands stuffed in her black leather jacket, a red scarf wrapped around her neck. She seems out of her element somehow. The lights and the music and the bustle are distracting everyone from looking at her and she resents it a little.

Now they're crossing the street and Kathy calls out and waves.

"Be careful, Sam. She's not telling you something. Something important," Kathy murmurs into my ear.

Lily sees us and waves back, her smile getting even bigger. Cindy's expression doesn't change. My head is spinning from the warmth of Cindy, the sweet scent of Lily and now Kathy's concern.

"Look what I found, Lily," Kathy squeezes my arm. "I think this belongs to you."

"No," Lily says, her smile turning down to just a

slight upturn of her mouth, looking at me. "Sam is all his own but sometimes he shares with me."

"Oh, Lily, that's so not true," Kathy says, pulling her arm away and pushing me gently towards Lily. "He's totally crazy for you, in his silent writer type way."

"Hey," I say, using Kathy's push to step forward.

"Hey," Lily says, taking my hand, which warms immediately at her touch.

"Hi, Kathy," Cindy cuts in. "Where is that lucky guy of yours?"

Kathy lights up like one of the Christmas trees in the park behind her.

"He's in Vancouver playing volleyball but he'll be home tomorrow night."

"That's great. I'm happy for the two of you."

Kathy keeps her smile up but her eyes are confused.

"Why care about me and Pete?" she asks, the brightness still in her voice. "You've got Lily and Sam and they're so wonderful together."

Cindy glances at me. That questioning look she gave me when we first met is still there but it is wary. It's like we have a history together but things went horribly wrong. She opens her mouth to reply to Kathy's question and it's like a cobra getting ready to spit venom. She has made her decision about me and it's not good. I wonder how she could feel all this about me since I haven't seen her since that day at the mall nearly three months ago. I suddenly realize Lily has been keeping me away from her, from her contempt for someone so clearly not good enough for her little girl. Lily has been carefully steering me out of her house whenever Cindy is due home. I feel manipulated, a cheap toy Lily has found in an empty lot and brought home but has to hide from mother.

I don't have time to be angry or hurt.

Before Cindy speaks, she looks at Lily and stops. Their eyes only meet for an instant, a blink. Nothing is said and the pause isn't even long enough for Kathy to notice but I catch a wave of Lily's scent. It's still her but it's rough and cold, like it's Christmas morning and someone is lying in their bed, trying to put on their happy face before going out to the family but they know what they want will never be found wrapped in gaudy coloured paper under a tacky fake tree.

"Oh, they are adorable," Cindy says, her cold smile in stark contrast to the heat coming off her.

"I hope you kids have a great time tonight," she adds. "Be safe."

She moves off quickly, heading down Abbott Street and away from the crowds. Kathy calls out a goodbye and then turns to us.

"God, Lily, your mom is so cool."

"Yeah, sure," Lily smirks, looking at me.

"Oooh," Kathy squeals. "Look at those cute little kids singing."

A wagon is pulling a children's choir slowly towards us. Their high young voices, the boys inseparable from the girls, soar delicately into the night air. The Trinity Baptist Children's Choir is printed in capital letters on a sign on the side of the wagon, which stops in front of us. A crowd quickly mills around, parents with video cameras, pushing Lily, Kathy and me together. The kids, no older than 10, start O Holy Night.

"This is one of my favourites," Kathy coos, cozying up next to me.

"A thrill of hope, a weary world rejoices, for yonder breaks a new and glorious morn."

Lily squeezes my hand. Her real scent is back, calm and soothing, pushing aside Kathy's warning and Cindy's rejection.

"Fall on your knees, oh hear the angels' voices."

A night divine.

It flew high into the sky,
Over our adoring faces,
And then it burst,
A flash of its purity,
Lighting our way,
Blinding.
And the pulse made all the lights go black,
And in the darkness, we began to burn.
It was beautiful.
Our screams like a choir,
Calling out in worship and praise.
Finally the songs of our destruction faded
And there was nothing left of us
Except for a dust falling like rain.
And the darkness consumed us
A wolf, alone on a mountain
Feeding
The dark blood of its prey
Sweet and thick as honey
In its throat.

Creation (Lily)

I stand outside his window in the dark.

I look around because I have the sensation I am not alone but I see no one else.

I do not feel the cold because I am warmed by his

proximity.

I want him to know me and know everything.

He is not like Samael and Amara and their followers, who saw humans as the final, intolerable evil, the corruption of guardians and the universe we are somehow supposed to maintain.

Samael sought me out because he wanted my help to purify creation, to make the universe clean again so the creator would return and reward us. I felt his desire, nurtured it, because I knew there would be a moment I would need it. He said words and made vows to me, just like I knew he was doing with Amara. I listened and I waited.

When Samael and Amara announced their plans to destroy humanity directly, by revealing themselves and exterminating them, Cindy intervened. She thought she could convince Samael to halt his plans but her earnest defense of humanity only made him turn against her. He threatened to eliminate her if she made any attempt to stop the eradication of the human filth.

I did not care then about the risk to me or Cindy and I do not care now.

Cindy does still care about my future and hers. And she knows what is going on with this Sam.

She wants me to deal with this problem.

She is furious with me for letting myself get close to another boy again so soon after the last time.

I just want him to survive.

He is human.

He is what I want.

I want.

Transition (Amara)

I walk to the edge of the water in a trance.

Behind me, the sun is setting.

Finally, the dark.

Samael.

I cannot wait to be with you.

Bodie believes I poured myself into our creation but I put more than that inside our little human Sam.

I let go of the little bit of dust of you I had held for so long. I put you into our creation so you could be reborn, so this Sam could be the best of you, and me, and Bodie.

The perfect weapon.

You have been away from me for so long. I hid in the dark for so long because I may have forgotten you if I had not.

Like you forgot about me.

I know you betrayed me for her at the end.

You could not resist her and she destroyed you.

I will make things right.

Destruction (Sam)

I can't answer the door because I have oven mitts on and I'm carefully pulling the turkey out of the hot oven under Mom's watchful eye. She holds her breath until I place the heavy pan safely on the counter.

"Good boy, Sam," she says like I'm five, moving past me to sweep off the foil and analyze the golden bird's baked carcass.

I tear off the mitts and walk towards the hall and the front door but I can already hear Dad.

"Cindy, please let me take your coat. Lily, you too."

"Oh, thank you, Arthur," purrs Cindy.

I walk around the corner and there's Cindy, pouring

herself out of a long black coat to reveal a shimmering red dress. Dad isn't doing any better this time than when we had run into her at the school's Christmas concert last week.

Kathy had an important role in some one-act play about the miracle of the holiday season and Lily was behind the scenes as the stage director.

When it was finally over, I got up with Mom and Dad, making our way towards the exit. They were exchanging Christmas greetings with some of the other parents they knew, even the ones they didn't like too much.

I needed to get outside. The closeness of the packed auditorium had nearly put me to sleep. I wanted to feel the sharp coldness on my face, making me awake and alert.

Along with the cold came Cindy's humid heat as soon as I cleared the doorway.

She was standing a few feet away, looking up at the sky thoughtfully.

"Hi, Cindy," I said as friendly as I could, walking over to her. After the frigid reaction she had given me the last time we met, I wanted to impress her, show her that her daughter's guy wasn't a total dud.

"Hello, Sam," she turned to face me. "While we're alone here, I just want to clear something up. My friends call me Cindy but I would prefer if you call me Cynthia."

I swallowed, trying to stay as cool as her voice was.

"Sorry…um, yeah, sure."

What a bitch.

"Did you see the concert, Cynthia?" I asked carefully.

"No, just got here," she said in a clipped tone. It was the voice of someone uninterested in making conversation.

"Oh." Any confidence I had was gone, leaving me a

nervous pile of babble. "That's too bad. You should have seen Kathy. She was fabulous as the old lady. Lily did amazing directing. Everything was right on time."

I just kept filling the air with jabber spewing from my mouth. Cindy or Cynthia or Her Royal Highness was politely nodding, so I couldn't stop, even when her eyes made it so clear she wanted to be anywhere except standing here in the cold, listening to me. Suddenly, she looked past me.

"Oh, you must be Sam's parents," she said to the man and woman coming up from behind.

There was an awkward silence as Mom and Dad came to a stop beside me. They were both staring at the busty blonde model in front of them who seemed to know their son. Normally, Dad was a ridiculous, embarrassing shameless flirt with the other school moms, heaping praise and attention on them. Now he just stood there in awe, staring.

Mom could usually be counted on in this kind of situation, so outgoing and friendly, always like Kathy in public. Like Dad, she just stood there. Cindy was looking at me expectantly.

Right.

"Uh, yeah, Mom and Dad. This is Lily's mom, Cynthia," I said, stilted with the introductions. "Cynthia, these are my parents, Art and Anna Gardner."

Cindy smiled and held her hand out to Mom.

"Anna, please call me Cindy. It really is a pleasure to meet you."

Now Dad's hand.

"Arthur, I've heard so much about you both from Lily."

Now turning to me, smiling brilliantly.

"You've both raised such a polite son. He is so attentive to Lily."

Both Mom and Dad came to consciousness at the same moment. Mom heaped some more praise my way while Dad slapped my shoulder in agreement. Now Mom was clucking away about how wonderful Lily was. I wasn't sure which Mom liked more—her son having a girlfriend hanging around the house or the girlfriend herself. Mom adored Lily, showering her with motherly affection whenever she was over. Lily turned on the charm in reply. One Sunday afternoon, I came home from the comic book shop to find the two of them making cookies and talking about baking techniques.

"Lily told me last week that the two of you aren't going anywhere for the holidays."

"Yes, that's right," Cindy answered politely. "I have two expectant mothers that will need me between Christmas and New Year's."

"Well, why don't you two come over for Christmas dinner?" Dad suddenly said loudly.

"Oh, yes," Mom gushed in support. "You must come over. We'll have plenty and it would be so nice to get to know you."

Cindy looked at Mom and Dad, then met my eyes for a second, as if she was appraising all three of us. She looked back at my parents, already smiling.

"Well, that would be lovely, Arthur. Please, Anna, let me bring a salad and some wine."

And now, 10 days later, she calls Dad Arthur again, a name I had only heard Grandma in Ontario call him. Mom would use that name on those rare occasions when she was looking for a large blunt object to kill him with. When either of the two main women in Dad's life called him Arthur, he would just stand there with this sour-milk look on his face and take whatever abuse was about to come his way as best he could.

Except now, he glows in pride as Arthur rolls out of Cindy's mouth like a caress. He stares at her for a long second in a way no son ever wants to see his dad stare at another woman, especially at the mother of his girlfriend. Naturally, Cindy looks radiant in her red dress, filling it out as indulgently as the wrapper on a handmade chocolate.

Dad only remembers his manners when Lily hands him her green coat.

"Here ya go, Art," she sings in a tease he doesn't pick up.

"Thank you, my dears," he says, hanging up the coats quickly on the hooks by the door. "Sam, make yourself useful for a second and take the wine and the salad from these lovely ladies and bring them into the kitchen."

Make yourself useful. I guess that makes Dad feel more masculine and in control to put me down in front of our guests. Lily holds out the bottle of red in one hand and a dark blue ceramic bowl with plastic wrap on the top in the other hand. I smile at her nervously but she just grins back as if this is going to be the best Christmas ever. I just hope to survive dinner.

And I do, of course. Even Sara behaves herself, although I think that's because she's mesmerized by Cindy, who gives her far more attention than she deserves, asking her about school and her friends and teasing her about boys. I watch Cindy carefully for the iciness she threw my way before but there's no sign of it now. She has Mom and Dad in stitches with some odd stories about dealing with anxious pregnant women and the idiot doctors who get in her way. I eat quietly, sneaking glances at Lily and laughing when I'm supposed to. Christmas cheer and all that whatever.

The food is great but there's no way I'm sitting for seconds at this table. I excuse myself and head into the kitchen to start cleaning up. This is a day I won't mind spending the next three hours, or however long Cindy is here, tidying up. While it seems her beauty and presence puts everyone else first speechless and then ridiculously at ease, it's Cindy's words that put me on edge and leave me there. It sounds like she's saying lines in a play, going for the audience reaction, but the person behind the persona is watching with detached boredom, waiting for something to happen. I realize that, in a strange way, I appreciate Cindy's coolness to me. It's honest, at least.

In front of my family, Cindy is perfect. Too perfect. Even her compliments towards me have Sara nodding and smiling in approval. There's only so much of this I can take. Off to the kitchen to start the dishes and pack up the leftovers. It's not Christmas unless you're eating leftovers until New Year's.

Lily is right behind me. She's starting to know her way around this kitchen pretty well, so we don't talk as we work. I'm more relaxed now that Cindy's voice is lost in the clatter of dishes and cutlery and Dad's frequent barking laugh.

I even make coffee and put the dessert on plates for Lily to serve. Dad looks at me like someone has kidnapped his son and left this butler disguised as his kid. He even grunts a thank you when I bring him seconds on the dessert and coffee without him even asking me to. Mom is flush with pleasure from the meal, the wine and the compliments on her cooking. She looks like she's going to burst with pride as I take away the remaining dishes and hustle back to the kitchen. Sara just sits on her butt, of course, but for this once I'm grateful.

As I close up the dishwasher and press the start button, I hear a ringtone in the dining room. Lily walks past me to the others and I follow. Cindy is casually standing off in the corner, murmuring into a cell. She turns and mouths a sorry to Mom and Dad while still listening.

"Don't apologize. I'll be there in 10 minutes." She flips the phone shut.

"I'm sorry but it seems one of my clients is having contractions. I'm sure they're premature because she's not due for another week but I would like to quickly check on her."

"Clients?" Mom asks.

"Oh, yes," Cindy smiles, heading for the hallway. "I can't call them patients because I'm not a doctor and they're not sick."

"Oh, of course," Mom laughs in understanding.

"Sam and I can come along," Lily volunteers.

"That would be wonderful," Cindy replies.

Lily herds me down the hall. I'm not keen on being around Cindy but hopefully it will be okay with Lily there. As Lily and I head to the hall to get our coats and boots, I grab my coat and boots, I can hear Cindy, apologizing for interrupting dinner and promising to bring back another bottle of wine.

"Go, go, go, duty calls," Mom urges.

"Maybe she just had too much Christmas dinner," Dad adds.

Everyone laughs except for me. I just shake my head at Dad's sad attempt at humor and head out the door.

Lily urges me into the back seat of their huge SUV

with her while Cindy gracefully climbs into the driver's seat and fires up the engine. She waves to my parents standing at the door and pulls out of the driveway. She drives quickly down Woodlawn to Springfield and turns right.

Lily grabs my hand. "Hang on," she warns.

My head snaps back and my body slumps into the plush leather seat as Cindy's dress shoe pushes the accelerator to the floor. I can see the needle fly past 60, 80, 100 kilometres an hour as we roar up Springfield, passing the few cars that are out on Christmas night like they are pylons.

I glance at Lily. This mad woman is driving like this is a race track and there isn't any black ice on the street to send us sliding into a light pole. Lily is smiling softly at me. She puts a finger to her lips for me to be quiet. I take a deep breath and look between Cindy's hand and the steering wheel, where I can spot the speedometer. The needle is gone, somewhere in the area I can't see past 130.

I check my seatbelt as we sail past Burtch and then Spall. The side of Cindy's face is calm and her hands are sure on the steering wheel but that doesn't slow my breathing, which is coming out in little gasps.

We slow down to 70 and Lily grabs my arm with a firm grip I never would have imagined from her delicate hands. We turn left onto Banks sharply, sailing through a red light but no one is coming. Even with Lily holding my arm, my head still jerks over and lightly thumps into the window. As Cindy straightens out and accelerates again, Lily lets go of my arm and looks away, stifling a laugh.

I'm about to complain until I see that Cindy is not slowing for the red light at Harvey. Great. One of the busiest intersections in Kelowna and she's about to blow through a red on it. A van crosses in front of us an instant before we get there. We fly across, about a second in front of the next vehicle coming into the intersection.

I blow out the trapped air in my lungs in relief. We cross Enterprise and charge towards Dilworth Mountain. Taking one hand off the wheel, Cindy hits the switch to open her window. The roar of the wind blows in along with the cold December air. The sharpness of the cold swirling through the SUV takes my mind off the road. Lily holds my arm again as we fly around a couple of more corners before screeching to a stop in front of a large, well-lit home.

Cindy is out and halfway up the step to the front door before I can speak.

"I thought this lady was having contractions or whatever. I mean, what the hell was that? Was she trying to kill us? Jeez, Lily, seriously, that was screwed up."

"Sssshhh," Lily says, gently, stroking my leg and looking at Cindy. A man answers the door and Cindy pushes past him inside. "Cindy feels terrible about leaving your parents after such a nice night but she also needs to be here so she's trying to get done what she needs to do as fast as she can."

"And kill us all in the process?" I protest, my voice too nervous and loud in my ears.

"Cindy's a good driver," Lily pats my leg in reassurance.

I look away, out the window, mad at Lily for the first time ever. I sit there, stewing, angry about everything. I don't like Lily blowing me off for being so scared to go flying down icy city streets at speeds you weren't even allowed to go on the highway. I'm angry at Cindy for driving that way and for being so cool towards me. I'm stressed about Christmas with my family. It just seems to be all piling up.

Lily's scent, normally so calming to me, seems too close, oppressive, intruding into my head. And Cindy's heat is still flooding the car but in a soggy, stale way, like she had been here once, a long time ago, and all that's left is this pathetic echo. Together, the smell and the warmth are making it hard to breath.

I ignore Lily, looking across the street at the Christmas decorations on some of the other houses, trying to calm down, breathe more slowly.

Inside the house directly across from us is a five-year-old boy, playing in his room with all his new toys. The door is shut but he can still hear his parents arguing in hushed tones downstairs. The presents are nice but what he really wants is for mom and dad to be happy with him and with each other. The boy's mother wants to escape, to get away from this house that's more like a prison, this husband who controls her and this child, always so needy, that she never wanted to begin with. And the boy's father wants his wife to just die, right now, and make his life easier, quieter, simpler. The depth of his desire to kill his wife is frightening. I know the carving knife in the sink would fit right in his hands.

I throw open my door and stumble out of the SUV, falling to my hands and knees on the brittle snow, gasping.

In the next house is a grandfather who can't stop looking at his nine-year-old granddaughter in a way that excites him and makes him feel like a monster at the same time. The old man's wife wants her daughter-in-law to stop being so bossy. Things were so much happier before her boy married that bitch.

In the house with Cindy is a woman who just wants the pain to stop and the baby to get out. She wants her body back because this pregnancy thing absolutely sucks. She had wanted it so bad and now that she has it, she wants it all to go away. They tried so hard to have a baby, for years, and nothing worked, and the doctors couldn't help but then they met Cindy in Vancouver and everything changed. They even moved here so Cindy could follow the pregnancy through. This woman wants the little life inside her, she wants to be a mother, but the sickness and the fatigue have left her so weak and helpless.

I'm gagging, choking, trying not to leave the recently eaten turkey and stuffing and green beans and carrots and gravy and apple pie in a steamy mess on this front lawn in front of the house of these rich people, whoever they are.

Lily runs to my side and bends down, asking me if I'm ok, but I can barely hear her over the racket as the wants and the needs and the desires of everyone on the block pour into my head, everyone dreaming and begging and pleading and fantasizing and plotting all at the same time. I push her hand away, off my shoulder, and moan. What's happening to me? Dreaming about feeling other people's wants is hard enough but I'm awake now. How can this be happening while I'm awake?

As I try to hold these voices and feelings back, I imagine I'm going to wake up any moment, lying in my bed, gritting my teeth, hands wrapped tightly around the sheets. I'll get up to sit at my desk and think about fire and angels and blood and despair and destruction and death. I won't write a word but my hand will ache, gripping the pen so hard. Just one more minute and I'll open my eyes, safe in my bed.

Instead, I catch my breath and look down at my hands

on the snow. My fingers have curled and are pushing their way down towards the frozen ground beneath. The air moving in and out of my throat makes scraping sounds. My ears feel like they're bleeding but now I can hear Lily beside me, the sound of a car on the next street, the whisper of a breeze on the trees behind the house. I can taste how close my dinner came to leaving me.

And I can smell Lily. Like always. I can feel her perfect, sweet scent, soaking softly into me. She wants me to be better, to be Sam again, her Sam. She wants to hold my hand and me to smile at her. She wants to listen to my voice. She wants to love me and stay with her forever.

I look at her and shiver. There's sweat on my face but I'm cold.

She smiles, hopefully.

"Did you get car sick?" she asks, hesitant.

"Yeah, sure," I say, pushing myself to my feet. I sway a second and then catch my balance. Lily puts her hand on my arm, an even tighter grip than when we were driving here.

"No. I don't know. I'm not sure," I mumble.

"C'mon," her hand is urging me back into the car. "Let's get you inside and warm you up."

"Ok."

Lily opens the front passenger door and holds my arm like I'm an old man as I slide into the seat. She shuts the door firmly, quickly moving around the SUV, closing the back doors and jumping into the driver's seat. She starts it up and flips a few knobs on the dash, flooding the inside with warmth. The hot air and the lights on the dash make me feel better. I sigh, breathing easier.

I feel calm and Lily is close, making me safe, but my skin feels like it's still too tight. My heart thuds in my head, keeping time to the swirl of thoughts flying around.

"Better now?" she asks, gently. The back of her hand comes up to touch my cheek.

I look at her and I feel like crying.

"Better than ever," I smile.

A snake, she wrapped her arms around me
And she took a bite from my face,
Her teeth sinking into me like bread
She chewed enthusiastically
Closing her eyes in satisfaction
She squeezed harder
I couldn't breathe
She pushed her mouth to mine
And I had all the air I would ever need.

Crucible (Lily)

As I run to his side, I am confused by what is happening.

Sam knows me now while he is awake and he is still here.

He should already be dead but he is so alive.

He knows I am no dream.

He is on his hands and knees in the snow, looking so weak and human.

I burst with compassion for him.

He is so fragile.

And Cindy will have felt his awareness of those people. His awareness of me.

She will end his life.

She hates him, just like she despised Samael so long

ago.

As I bend down to attend to Sam, I remember what was said and what I did.

You are in the dark so you do not see what you are, Cindy had told Samael at their last meeting. He just smiled and said he was the shadow of all things.

He threatened to destroy her if she got in the way of his plans to exterminate the humans.

Cindy laughed.

"Destroy me? How can you destroy the act of creation?"

Without a word, Amara attacked. Some others they had befriended—Cherry, Ruby, Kyle and Dan—joined in.

And for the first time, a guardian felt pain.

The five of them were ripping Cindy apart.

I could hardly bear to watch but I knew I had to wait. Like the guardian of death, some of us had decided to let go of our voice and our physical presence but I had never seen someone forced away, torn into tiny pieces. As they intensified the attack, I came to believe it was possible.

Cindy began to fade.

I went to Samael. He was absorbing Cindy's suffering with earnest.

"Samael," I asked. "Do you still want me?"

He flooded me with his dark.

"More than ever."

"I know," I answered.

And I let him in.

And I have let Sam in.

But he is not like the others.

He is not Samael.

I can feel it.

Fruition (Amara)

I lie back in the sand
And wait for the dark to
Engulf me in its arms
A babe about to nurse
A shark about to feed
Escaping from this curse
Satisfying my need
Finally safe from harm
Finally back on land.

When the eyes of my eyes see (Sam)

My stomach has calmed but my brain is still hot and boiling over by the time Cindy comes out of the house about 10 minutes later. She climbs into the back seat where Lily had been sitting on the way over.

"Is everything alright?" she says as Lily puts the SUV into gear and pulls away, driving like a normal person would.

"Yes, Cindy. Sam wasn't feeling well so we came to sit in the front." Lily's voice is too smooth to my ears, annoying me by how she's brushing away what happened.

"That's too bad," replies Cindy in a tone that lets me know she really doesn't give a crap.

"How was your client?" Lily asks.

"Ms. Jacobsen will be fine. She won't go into her real contractions for another three days. She is nervous and tired but she will sleep better tonight. I'll call her tomorrow to make sure she stays calm."

I can't understand why I'm so angry. The more they talk, the more focused I become. I can feel my thoughts, exact as razors, on my tongue and then out into the air.

A small part of me is somewhere else, watching, quiet and ready.

"So why did we have to drive here like that then?" I say quietly.

"Sam…" Lily puts her hand on mine again. I grab her wrist and guide her hand quickly back to the steering wheel.

"Both hands, please," I say.

"No, Lily. Let the boy speak. I prefer it when he speaks his mind," comes Cindy's patronizing voice from the back.

"Cindy…" Lily says quickly. A warning.

"Let the boy speak?" I mimic, my voice still low but sharp with rage. "That's rich. You drive like a maniac, I get sick and my reward is I get to speak. Fantastic."

"As I said, that's too bad," Cindy's voice oozes, even more callous than before, if that was possible.

I can feel Lily's scent washing over me, trying to settle me and sweep away my anger. Instead, it's just fuel to a fire I feel behind my eyes.

"Stop that," I say to Lily. "Whatever you're doing with your smell, stop that. Stop trying to control me, telling me what I want."

Lily's fingers flex, squeezing the steering wheel. She closes her eyes for a long second and then opens them again. What was once soft has now become something distant and sad. In the back, I hear Cindy draw in a sharp breath.

"Lilith, you will drive us to our home. This cannot be allowed. We must act immediately," Cindy orders.

Lily sighs. There is so much sorrow in the release of the air from her lungs and the sound it makes that I want to throw myself from the SUV, hoping the back tires will run me over in the process. My rage runs over her misery like a speed bump.

"What the hell are you talking about?" I demand. "What's going on here?"

"You know too much already, young man," Cindy replies. Her humidity, mixed in with Lily's scent, is a sweet cocktail that only seems to make me more confident to speak, throwing out shards of glass from my head into the air.

"Alright, what's the deal with you two? Lily, I dream about you almost every night but you're not you. You're that smell, that perfume, and you're inside everyone in my dreams, making them want things and crave things, nice things, terrible things. How come I can know that smell even from far away? How come I feel this heat from you, Cindy? How come I know you're coming even before I see you? How come the two of you seem to just wrap everyone you meet around your finger, especially you, Cindy or Cynthia, whatever the hell your name is? How come you just look at people and talk to them and touch them and they respond to you that way?"

The road is slipping away, black and quiet underneath us. We're getting close to their house but I can't stop spilling my thoughts. It's energizing, like I'm clearing the air from all those sensations I've been absorbing from both of them for the last few months. I feel I'm walking into a cleansing shower first thing in the morning, waking me up.

"Cindy, you know what I'm talking about. When I first met you, that day at the mall, I knew you were coming from a mile away. I could feel you there. And Lily, too. And then you did something to Pete and Kathy. You touched them. Both at the same time. And they've been together since, like you made them see what they felt for each other, pushed them together."

"Sam, Sam…" Lily tries to cut in, pleading. We're turning down Rose. Their house is there on the left.

"Lily, what was all that crap you said to me when we met about being a harvester of ideas and having a gift?" I shout out.

Cindy is already getting out of the SUV, even as it's still rolling to a stop in the driveway.

"You spoke to him? You let him hear your real voice? Lilith, what were you thinking?" Cindy yells at Lily.

"I'm sorry," Lily says, killing the motor.

I'm already jumping out. I take quick strides around the front of the SUV to confront the two of them. I'm ready to settle this right now. By the time I get there, Lily is standing to one side, looking down. Cindy is facing me squarely, her hands knotted in balls at her side. Her eyes are narrow, drilling into me.

"In the house," she commands.

"You can't boss me around," I bellow back at her.

Lily looks up at me. The sadness is gone from her. There's something rough and wild there, reflected from the street lights.

"Now, Sam," she orders in a whisper, that same whisper she had talked to me with when she had picked up my poetry and looked at it. A voice, old and sure.

I turn to the front of the house and walk to the door. What's happening? I'm so confused. All that anger seems to have been snuffed out. Now I'm just doing what she tells me to do, with no choice at all. I feel ridiculous for having said everything I did, yet I know I'm not wrong. There seems to be so much more going on than me saying all those crazy fantasies and dreams that had been in my head about them. And why did I say those things? Where's the idiot who said all that stuff? He's made a run for it and left me here to pick up the mess.

The door is unlocked. I walk in, turning to my right into the dark living room. The only light in the room is coming from outside, sneaking through the thin drapes of the front window.

The door closes behind me with a click.

The lights stay off.

There's a rush of movement, a cold wind suddenly gusting across an empty street, stirring dead leaves. I'm swept up and slammed against the wall with such force the windows shake. I gasp but I can't breathe. The impact compresses my ribs, forcing every last ounce of oxygen out of my lungs.

Cindy's body is pressed against me, pinning me to the wall, her left hand on my throat, her right hand firmly on my shoulder. Her face is inches from mine. She is smiling like a predator.

"And now, Sam, what do you see? What do you feel?" she breathes.

I look at Lily but she isn't there. I blink fast but I can't believe what I'm seeing. There's just a soft light in the shape of her body standing halfway across the room. Her eyes burn as she looks not at me but through me. I have to look away but Cindy grabs my jaw and yanks it back so hard I feel bones protest in my neck.

"Lilith, he sees," she whispers, with surprise and wonder in her voice.

"I know," Lily says, stepping forward to Cindy's side.

I squeeze my eyes shut but Lily still shines through and now Cindy, too, filling my head with their light. I moan and my eyes open in surrender, looking up past them, into the world. Lily's gentle scent is everywhere, in everything, over the water and the land and the people and everything alive. Cindy's wet musk is mixed in. Cells are combining, then separating, animals mating, a mouth opening and singing the sweetest song, all generating her heat. I see Pete and Kathy kissing roughly, their breath in panicked gasps. Lily and Cindy's essence is swirling around them.

Beyond them, I can feel my parents, my sister, people from school and a faceless horde beyond them, all looking at me, smelling so perfect, so warm and moist in their humanity. Mom waves. Sara shakes her head in slow disgust, as if I'm finally coming to realize something she knew all along.

Now they are all pressing forward, marching into my head, all at once, all of their yearnings and I know it's making me scream but I can't hear over the burning in my head, the pressure behind my eyes.

"Sam."

Lily presses her hand against my forehead.

It's cool.

The room is dark and quiet again, except for the sound of my erratic gasps. I'm too scared to cry.

Lily's next to me, looking like she always looks, compact and perfect. She smiles but Cindy's hold on me never wavers.

"Cindy, why are you hurting me?" I moan, never looking away from Lily.

"Because you're an abomination," Cindy starts but Lily cuts her off angrily.

"Don't call him that," she hisses.

"It's what he is. Isn't that right, Sam?" Cindy replies, rolling my name out of her mouth like a curse.

"Stop," I beg. "What's she talking about, Lily? What is this?"

"I'm afraid we're long past questions, boy," Cindy says. "Your vision is a threat to us and we cannot allow it. I am doing this for your own good. Your madness is already taking over and then you will attract the others. That must not happen."

"But—" I stare at Lily, not understanding.

Lily takes my hand and squeezes it tight.

"I'm so sorry, Sam," she sobs, her eyes open wide and wounded. "I never wanted this to happen. I'm so sorry."

Lily lowers her head and puts her other hand gently on Cindy's shoulder.

Cindy's right hand plunges into my chest.

I feel the ripping of skin and nerves, the shattering of bones.

Now both of her hands, ripping me apart, making a noise like when Dad splits logs in the backyard with the axe, a crunching protest as the wood separates.

I'm not dying. Instead, I feel a pressure in my chest so tight but now gone. My breath, which I could not catch before, is now a huge sigh, an exhale of pent-up energy, a sexual release that floods me.

There is a scream but it's not me.

It's Cindy, who steps back like she's dunked both hands into bubbling acid, howling in surprise.

Lily lunges forward and forces her hands into the wreckage of my chest.

There's a wet, mashing sound. Her face tightens in effort and she falls back quickly, nearly falling.

In her hands is a raw red steak the size of a grapefruit.

It shivers, spraying blood.

Once.

Twice.

And then it stops.

She looks at me.

I can't understand her face.

Mixed in with a strange relief is shock and horror. I don't know whether she wants to take me into her arms or run for her life.

Cindy is much easier to read.

She still wants me dead but she is now confused about how to go about it.

Her hands, covered in my blood, are tight fists at her side.

I look at both of them and smile.

My hands come up and cover the black hole in my chest where my heart used to be.

Attraction (Amara)

He is so beautiful and the effort to not run to his side is excruciating.

I stand by the car, looking across the street at the house, my feet ready to fly.

And then it happens.

He is Samael but he does not know himself.

"I tried to tell you but you would not listen," Bodie says, behind me. "You have released forces you do not understand, Amara. Did you honestly believe I would not know you put your remnants of Samael in him?"

I turn to him, frustrated.

"And—?"

"No, Lilith has not taken control of him. Your weapon is still intact. He still has all of the ability to deliver the outcome you seek. He has not shed his humanity yet, however."

The full moon breaks the cloud cover and its light makes everything blue and mysterious. I stare at Bodie and he just smiles back at me.

"Do not worry," he says, walking away from me and around the car to the driver's side. The car's lights are on and I can hear its motor idling. "He will not be human for much longer. There are too many temptations before him."

"And then?" I enter the car and take my place in the seat next to him. I am numb.

Bodie takes my face in his hands.

"Be patient," he says gently. "You do not need to go to him. He will come to you."

"Will you go to her now?" I ask. My voice is shaking.

"She will find me."

He drives away carefully but I do not care.

A sound is coming from my mouth and I am shocked to discover it sounds like laughter.

I am ecstatic.

How we came to be at this moment (Lily)

Samael's desire and his yearning made me squeal with delight.

As his disciples attempted to murder Cindy, his darkness spread through me. He wanted so much and in the deepest part, I found his last longing.

He wanted everything to fall into him.

He wanted to consume not just humanity but all of the guardians and even Amara herself. He would betray them all to get what he desired. He sought the stillness and quiet of himself to be all that was left. He believed he alone was the nothingness of the creator.

If he could restore existence to this state, to himself, he honestly thought the creator would reunite with him, the most loyal disciple.

In that moment, I understood who could bring what Samael sought. He did not understand how the dark was still a place, a state of being. What the guardian of death brought was the absence of the dark and all else. She brought the true void, the emptiness, the nothingness, not him.

So I laughed at him.

Samael believed he was devouring me in him as the flood of his endless wants percolated through me.

So I let him all the way in.

And then I closed the door.

The assault on Cindy stopped.

Amara and the others turned to me. Cindy slowly rose to her feet, bloody and torn, a horrible smile of understanding spilling from her broken human face.

I held out my arm and opened my hand towards Amara. A black marble sat there.

"No," Amara begged me. "No."

I closed my hand and brought the fist to my lips, kissing it.

And then I opened my hand and blew the ashes out.

They all evaporated before Amara.

I heard the giggle of a little girl.

I walked past Amara to Cindy and took her into my arms.

Bodie took Amara away, to explain to her what had happened, how Samael had been taken from her.

Devastation (Amara)

When Bodie speaks of my love's end, there is no mention of loss. There is only a story, a string of words, which is supposed to add up to knowledge of the event.

Bodie has admitted to me that is the best he can do. His knowledge cannot cross over into faith, nor can it incorporate the feeling of experience. He knows of Samael's ending because he was there to witness it but he did not experience it. He did not love Samael. The moment Samael dissolved was another instance of learning for Bodie but for me it was the loss of a large part of me. I miss him so much.

Lilith did that to me.

The others hate Lilith for her betrayal but she was only protecting herself and Cindy. I accept her, my cunning sister.

I despise Samael for being so weak to expose himself to her, for letting his wants betray him.

He was so ignorant of her power. He was so stupid. At the moment I was ready to eliminate Cindy, humanity's matriarch, and end their plague upon our universe, my great gift to my love, Samael was gone.

Lilith had the power to just stop him but she did not. Instead, she erased him and left me with the pain of his passing.

This new development, this Sam I have constructed, is gorgeous, a surprising sweetness at the bottom of my bitter cup. He will leave her side and come to me.

Lilith will know what it is to be weak and to suffer before the end.

Healing the hole (Lily)

Sam holds out his hand.

"I think you have something that belongs to me," he says quietly, looking at the bloody mess in my hands.

I look down at it. There isn't much light but I can see that it is indeed a human heart. There is no deception here. So what is Sam? If he is not human, what is he? How has he come to be?

"Do not give it to him, Lilith. We do not know what he is," Cindy hisses.

"I don't know what I am, either," he replies before I can. "But I don't want to fight. I just want my heart back."

"Even though we tried to kill you," I say. I can't hold his eyes. It's the hole in his chest that has my attention. That dark in there isn't like the dark around us in this room. It's a dark I had held once, long ago.

"Even though you tried to kill me," he agrees.

"Are you the human Sam?" I need to know. Cindy is still tensed for a battle.

The smile fades from his face.

"Yes," he says slowly.

"No," he looks down and shakes his head.

"I don't know. I'm not sure," he looks back at me. I can feel his sincerity. There is confusion in his eyes.

Most of all, I can feel no malice in him, no desire to attack us. He simply wants his heart back. He wants us to trust him.

I step forward.

"LILITH!" Cindy shouts.

"Hush. He means us no harm."

"This isn't right."

"No, it certainly is not. We shall have answers but first…"

I hold out the heart to Sam.

"Put it where you found it," he says, staring at me intently.

I look from his eyes to that terrible hole in his chest. His shirt is torn and stained with blood. The top of his rib cage is shattered. I can see jerky movement inside. It's his lungs working.

I look back to his face. He is smiling again, my Sam. This boy has no idea the effect he has on me. What I would do for him.

I step forward and push my hands into his chest cavity. Cindy has moved right behind me in a defensive stance. My hands burn and I yank them away, startled. Cindy grabs my shoulders and pulls me back.

Neither of us move as Sam's eyes close. He sighs and then collapses. His head hits the carpet with a thud and he is still.

I kneel at his side. His shirt is still ruined but his chest is whole again, as if he was never wounded. He is breathing softly. He will regain consciousness momentarily.

"Lilith, we are in danger. We must run," Cindy says, her hand touching my shoulder.

"Yes, we are in danger but no, I will not run. Not until I know the full extent of the threat."

"It could be too late by then," she protests.

"Hush. He wakens."

She squeezes my shoulder.

His breathing hitches and his eyes flutter open, trying to focus. They grow alert, spinning around the room until they find my face.

"Lily?"

"I'm here, Sam." I put my hand on his chest.

He looks down at my hand on his skin. His eyes widen as he sees what remains of his shirt.

"Whoa…" He gasps. "What?" He looks at me and then over my head as he realizes Cindy is there.

He tries to move but I push softly. I can feel the warmth of his skin, the lungs taking in and expelling air, the heart beating. He is whole.

He takes a deep breath and relaxes. He is drawing in my scent. I had been blind to how thorough an effect my presence has on him but now I am aware. I can feel his senses absorbing me. It is intoxicating.

"So…um…are you going to tell me how I ended up lying down on your living room floor with a torn shirt? And what's all that wet gunk all over your hands?"

Cindy moves away to turn on a light. I am helping Sam to his feet as a lamp comes on.

"Whoa. Is that blood?" He sees my hands. They are already drying but I have left marks on his chest.

Under the light, the blood is everywhere. It is all over his pants, my clothes, Cindy's clothes, the floor.

"What happened here?" His voice rises in panic. His breathing quickens as his head jerks around the room.

"You don't remember?" Cindy says, coming back to my side.

He looks at her warily.

"I remember going to the lady's house with the labour pains. I remember arguing about your driving coming back here. And…" he pauses, looking away from us, down to the floor where a huge stain of blood is soaking into the light carpet.

"And I told you how you made me feel." He does not look up. His voice is distant, like he is trying to recall a faded memory. "And you were mad at me and took me here. And then, no, I don't remember…"

He looks back at us, hoping we will accept the lie.

"Tell us what you don't remember," Cindy says. Her voice is fierce and hot beside me.

He looks at her and shivers.

"Cindy, you will not speak to Sam in this manner," I warn her. "You must be patient."

"LILITH," Cindy growls through clenched teeth, glaring at me.

"Hey, that voice," Sam brightens. "You talked that way when you read my notebook and when…"

He stops again. Now he is staring at me, scared.

"What is it?"

"You and Cindy…"

His voice is sad. He looks down at his feet. "You tried to kill me."

I rush forward and wrap my arms around him. "I'm sorry, Sam. I'm so sorry," I whisper into his shoulder.

He tenses and his arms stay at his side.

"You tried to kill me."

Cindy snorts. "We did kill you. But, for some reason, you're not dead."

I take his face into my hands and force him to look at me.

"Sam, I'm happy you are alive. I did not wish to harm you but the circumstances forced us to do what we did."

"What circumstances? You're freaking me out. What happened?" He pulls away from me sharply.

I catch his arm, stopping him abruptly. He tries to pull away again but I hold him calmly.

"Lily… Stop it. Stop… Let me go."

He punches my wrist with his free hand. He hits my arm again as hard as he can. Again. He looks at me, furious. Then the back of his open hand plows into my face, making a sharp slapping sound. I never look away. He strikes my face three more times, the last two with his fist. I do not blink.

He is crying now.

"Let me go," he shouts, covering his red face with his free hand.

I wrap my arms around him again and this time he falls into me, his body shaking.

I stroke the back of his head gently and kiss his neck.

"I am not hurt, Sam. You cannot injure me or Cindy physically. Please, Sam. I will answer all your questions. I can feel how much you want an explanation. Give me a chance. Please."

He pulls back and looks at me. His face tells me I have pulled his heart out again. He is aching over my betrayal and his pain is excruciating to me. I cannot bear his eyes. They are so angry and sad and confused and scared. He does not realize they are so much more powerful than his fists. I force myself to hold his stare because I deserve this pain, deserve his fury.

"Please," I beg. I want his understanding and his forgiveness across my whole being. I know if he walked away, I would fade right then. It would be so easy, waiting for the guardian of death to come and take me away, so Sam cannot hurt me anymore and I cannot hurt him.

"Please."

Sam sighs. "OK."

Cindy shakes her head and then falls heavily into a nearby armchair. Anger is pouring off her like steam.

He looks at her and then looks back at me.

"This is so fucked up."

His voice is warm and there might be a laugh somewhere close.

"I know," I breathe in relief. His eyes are soothing

again.

He sits down on the couch and pats the cushion beside him. I sit there.

Cindy takes a breath to speak but I hold my hand up and she stops.

"I will explain, Cindy, thank you." I turn to Sam. "As you saw in the moment before we tried to kill you, we are not human, Sam, although we are in human form. We are two of a species that has been in existence since the beginning of this universe. From time to time, some humans have been able to perceive us walking amongst you. We have never met anyone with your depth of perception before. You have seen us, you hear us, you sense us, and what we are, on a level we are not accustomed. You should be insane or dead by your own hand by now."

I pause. He's watching me but his eyes are cold and distant.

"So you tried to kill me out of pity?"

His words tear into me. I feel a sharp jab in my chest.

"Yes…and no," I murmur. "If you remember, your mind nearly became detached in the moment before we…I…tried to murder you."

"I remember." His voice is flat.

"But the real reason…" Cindy starts but I cut her off. He has to hear it from me. I have betrayed his trust.

"The real reason we needed to kill you," I say, my voice too loud, "is because you pose a threat to us."

"You tried to kill me in self-defence?"

"That's right," Cindy says.

"No, that's not quite right," I say, turning to glare at Cindy. She ignores me, staring at Sam. Although she's sitting, she's still tensed for a fight.

"Your perception of us," I continue, looking back at

Sam, "would have been…sorry, is a magnet that would have drawn others of our kind to you. You have seen too much of us, know too much about us. Inadvertently, you would have helped those that are looking for us discover us. We are…outcasts among many of our kind. Some are actively searching to find us and punish us."

Sam takes a deep breath and I can feel his mind drawing in not just me but Cindy, too. She twists in her chair angrily. We are used to our essence moving effortlessly through the consciousness of organic creatures but we have never experienced a human reaching into our sphere. His previous awareness of us was so small and brief that I had barely noticed it but this is intentional.

The sensation is intense and thrilling. I never thought I could experience Sam at this level. I enjoy his presence but I had believed our time together would be fleeting, like all of my past relationships with humans. I feel both relieved and excited to know he can see me, absorb me.

It also feels like a violation. I deeply understand Cindy's discomfort. Sam's probing awareness of us is invasive and there is no way we can stop it. If he desires, he can know us in all our aspects yet somehow remain separate. No guardian has that kind of access to another guardian. Even the shared link between Cindy and me has its limits.

"Stop it," Cindy growls. "Stop. That. Right. Now." She is trying to force him away but his mind is a wall of fog, creeping forward, covering everything in its path.

Startled, Sam shakes his head. "What? What did I do?"

Both of us feel the rush of movement inside. He was there, moving inexorably through us. His departure is sudden and sharp. Cindy looks down into her lap, her anger dissolving into a feeling of powerlessness. I feel unsettled, disturbed by how willing I would be to get lost in that fog, opening myself to him permanently.

"You lived," Cindy whispers. "That's what you did."

Before Sam can react or Cindy can say more, I jump in. "Sam, I know all of this is hard to understand but you should be dead. Because you are not dead, you are clearly something other than human."

"Or more than human," he says, looking at me with an empty expression on his face.

Cindy huffs, rises and walks out of the room.

I move to sit closer to him. I take his hand and hold it to my cheek, sighing and closing my eyes. He is taking in my scent again but more gently now, slower. A moment later, I hear the car door open and then slam shut. The motor roars and tires protest as Cindy speeds away. Her departure seems to take the tension out of the room with her. Sam feels safe and I am calm, even though I know I am taking a terrible risk to stay with him.

I cannot believe how I deluded myself. I wanted to believe Sam was somehow natural but I ignored how impossible he was and how there must be a guiding hand that led to our meeting. I see Amara stalking me now but I still do not see her intent.

My mind is filled with questions. What is Amara's purpose with Sam? Is he here to destroy us or to distract us? Does he pose a threat to humanity? Were we not supposed to find out Sam's true nature until a later time? What would happen now that Sam was aware of both of us and his own abilities? The many questions and the few answers frustrate me.

Worst of all, has Amara found our hiding place among the humans? Is she stalking us, biding her time as she amasses her forces against us for a final confrontation?

Sam's fingers on my face squeeze my cheek softly.

"You're in trouble, aren't you?"

I push the air out of my lungs. I surprise myself by starting to chew on the corner of my bottom lip absent-mindedly, the way I have seen so many girls at the school do.

I move my head in a slow nod.

I look at Sam. His eyes are gentle and concerned.

"That is the only thing of which I am sure, Sam."

He smiles. "I'm only sure that I really like that voice, your real voice." He looks down. "And I'm sure I need a new shirt."

Answers (Sam)

I should be dead.

Cindy and Lily tried to kill me.

I don't understand this.

I look at her and I want everything to be alright.

I touch her cheek and wonder how I'm alive.

I wonder if this is skin I really feel on her face or is it fake, a mask for what she really is?

I feel something inside of me that knows the answers.

Cindy and Lily are afraid.

I am not afraid.

Not anymore.

Certainty (Amara)

They all come to me, demanding we attack.

I am so calm and relaxed, I can barely contain my glee.

My plan is coming to fruition with even better results than I ever imagined.

Samael has returned and he will wipe this place clean.

I call Kyle and Dan to me. I smile at them. I am almost ready to shine again.

Kyle and Dan are eager when I explain the task I require them to complete.

"Hurt him but don't kill him? As you wish," Dan grins, cracking his knuckles.

I nod.

"Wait for my command."

He will come to me but he must be prepared first.

Questions (Lily)

While Sam speaks to his mother on the phone, I use a carpet steam cleaner to try and clean the blood out of the living room rug. It seems to be removing most of the redness but a stain is more than likely. The volume of the machine is drowning out most of Sam's words but I can still pick up the soothing tones as he tells his mother a perfect story about Cindy and her client, and how the two of us are at their house and he would be home later and not to worry.

The first Sam was able to tell stories effortlessly, too. His gentle voice and confident reasoning put many of the other guardians at ease. Amara and her cohorts adored how simple and perfect he made everything sound so they stopped hearing what he was actually saying. Ironically, he had exhibited a trait we had seen among many humans over the generations. Like him, they could say things so well and for so long that they came to believe they spoke truth, rather than simply an ardent desire.

Sam finishes his call and comes to help me with the rest of the cleaning. We do not speak as we wipe the walls. We wash our hands together in the kitchen sink. I disappear for a moment to change my clothes. When I emerge, I hand him a hoodie of Cindy's.

"You're almost the same size," I shrug.

"Just in different places," he smirks, handing me his ripped shirt to throw away.

The walls in the house are too close so we go for a walk; the cold quiet air seems to bring relief. We hold hands out of habit and I take comfort in the warmth of his skin. We wander aimlessly, talking only occasionally. When we speak, it is of other things—the weather, the light traffic, the sound of the water as we walk on a wooden pier at the lake.

After a time, we are standing in front of his house. The windows are dark except for a light in one window.

"Sara's on the computer," he says. "Nobody will see me. I'll ditch these pants and I'll get you Cindy's hoodie back tomorrow."

"Ok."

He steps forward quickly, his hands grabbing my arms. His mouth pushes into mine with an urgency he has never shown before. When we had kissed previously, I was the initiator. I meet his lips with my own passion. I cannot help myself. This boy, or whatever he is, could be the death of both me and Cindy but in his arms, my concern evaporates.

He pulls away as suddenly as he moved to me. The streetlight captures his smile as he quietly moves up the walk and lets himself in the house. He does not look back as the door closes quietly behind him.

I hear Cindy's SUV complain as she attacks the corner

at the end of the street. She had been close, watching and waiting. Now she is coming to pick me up so we can deal with this situation.

I step out into the middle of the street as the lights bear down on me. She does not slow down. Instead, she accelerates. She is probably going more than 100 kilometres an hour when the vehicle strikes me.

The impact makes a loud, metallic thump. My head crashes into the windshield as my body flips over the top of the speeding vehicle in a somersault. I land on my feet, soft as a cat, chuckling, and walk to the end of the street, where she has stopped. The vehicle is purring with menace, much like its driver.

"Do you feel better now?" I ask, climbing into the passenger seat.

"Yeah, right," she barks, slamming the vehicle into gear and pulling away.

"How are you planning to explain that big dent in the grille and the cracked windshield?" I laugh.

"Must have hit a stupid deer," she replies.

"Well, that is enough childish behaviour for one night," I scold her but not harshly. "We have much to do and I will have your complete attention, Cindy."

"As long as I have yours," she says, sailing into our driveway and killing the engine.

We enter the house and fall away from our human disguises so our essences can move freely.

A careful exploration of the human realm finds nothing amiss. Sam's dreams begin but they stay in the distance as usual. Cindy is upset with herself for not examining his dreams more closely when we first sensed them but I tell her I had also been fooled by what had appeared to be only a slight awareness by Sam of our true selves.

She does not respond but I can sense that she holds me largely responsible for this situation, that both my proximity and interest in Sam blinded me to the grave danger.

In the centuries since I had destroyed Samael, we had let ourselves beyond humanity only three times. Living among the humans is both an obvious hiding place and the last place Amara would spend any time looking. For her and her followers, we are hiding in the equivalent of a sewer and I thought they would not lower themselves so far to find us but I was obviously wrong. They came down to us and found us.

Our previous ventures in the broader universe had been brief and thoroughly planned. This will be much riskier. We both wonder if we are simply falling into the trap that has been laid for us. I assure Cindy that Sam's awareness of his situation is incomplete at best. He's not only ignorant of his power, he's in almost total denial. I will not be lulled into complacency by Sam's warm presence again. During our walk, he took several cautious breaths of my scent and I used the opportunity to gauge his thoughts. There was a significant part of his consciousness that refused to believe what had happened, particularly that I had tried to murder him and he had survived.

For the time being at least, this confusion is clouding any analysis on his part of what is the far more relevant issue for Cindy and me. His continued existence means he is something unique and powerful. There's no question he is still human but he's also something else. What is he, how has he become this way and what threat does it pose to us are the most pressing concerns.

Since Sam clearly does not know, and we must discover the answers before he comes to his own conclusions, we have to risk everything and let ourselves appear in the broader universe, beyond the comforting confines of humanity where we have remained in hiding.

Cindy wishes to confront the guardian of death but I discourage her from such a plan. The guardian of death has not spoken directly to anyone for more than half of all of time and would be unlikely to change policy now. The guardian has not been felt by us since Samael's end. So we are not even sure if the guardian of death could, or would, be perceived by us any longer. And we perceive all we need to know—Sam remains alive.

We need to know what our foes know and the only way to obtain that information with any confidence in its accuracy is simply to ask directly. Approaching Amara or any of her lieutenants is out of the question as they move together as a pack. We need to find a solitary guardian, one who remains on the periphery but is also in tune with Amara's agenda. Ideally, it is a guardian who will run and tell Amara about the encounter with us immediately after we retreat with the information we need. It is important for Amara to know that we are rising fearlessly and aggressively to her challenge, if that is what Sam represents.

There is only one guardian who meets such specific criteria.

Despite the risk and his fickle nature, it will be good to speak again with Bodie. I insist to Cindy that I go alone. Cindy's impatience and demanding nature will not give us the information we seek. The two of us together will be seen as a threat. While he would not directly deceive us, he would give us as little accurate information as he could, possibly leading us to the wrong conclusion as a result. I know he will respond to me if I come to him alone. I have always felt a special kinship with Bodie. When humans acquire the knowledge he possesses, it fuels further yearning. We can speak as equals, he will tell me what I need and he will inform Amara of our conversation as soon as I leave.

Reluctantly, Cindy agrees with my assessment. She suggests she reexamine our modest defences in the human realm for their continued effectiveness. I agree and encourage her to also locate but not contact the four guardians we believe may come to our aid if we call. If we require their assistance at a later time, it will save valuable energy at a time of crisis to already know where they are. She leaves me to carry out her mission.

Finding Bodie is often challenging and this time is no different.

My essence moves carefully through the known universe but still I cannot find him. He is not in any of the known places guardians come to be. I begin to wonder if Bodie is gone and I am filled with dread. The gaps in his knowledge may have inspired him to move on from this plane of existence and accept death.

I know he would never fight with us when the time came but he is a friend nonetheless. I can count on him to tell me the truth, especially if it is something I do not want to hear. He can be cruel but he is never wrong.

My thoughts drift back to Sam. I will have to trust Cindy more than ever. My feelings for him are affecting my judgment. I want to be with him and protect him from all of this but that is now impossible. Is he simply an aberration? His obliviousness suggests it but the timing and proximity to us make it unlikely. He is a weapon, a bomb dropped in our lap. When he comes to know his purpose, we must be prepared.

I need to know how to destroy him.

In my sadness, I cannot help myself. I approach the

edge of Sam's dreams, just to be near him.

Unexpectedly, Bodie is there.

I slip back into my human form and walk out the front door of the house. Cindy has not returned yet. It is late now, past 4 a.m. The sun will not rise for more than three hours. The streets are still. The sound of my boots on the icy sidewalk make a cold, scraping sound.

When I walk around the corner onto Sam's street, I see a car across the street from his house. Its lights are off but the car is running quietly. It is a big red convertible from the late 1960s, in perfect shape. The top is down, even though it is winter. Inside, an old man sits, wearing nothing but a loose muscle shirt, bright beach shorts and flip-flop sandals.

"Bodie."

"Pina colada?" he says, turning to me and holding out a frothy drink in a huge light blue glass.

I open the passenger door and sit beside Bodie, taking the drink. The smooth coconut flavor slips easily down my throat.

"This is nice," I say.

"Thank you. I'm glad you like it."

He flips his sunglasses down from the top of his head to cover his eyes and puts the car into gear. We drive away silently. Unlike Cindy, Bodie follows all the rules of the road, stopping at the appropriate lights, obeying all the signs. He heads down Water Street, through downtown. There is no one around to notice the oddity of a tanned and fit man in his 60s, dressed for Florida but driving a convertible in Canada on a below-freezing night in December.

We do not speak as he takes the turn at the end of the street, charging up Knox Mountain. We are in the dark now, away from the lights of the city. I can barely make out the road but he obviously can, even through his sunglasses, steering confidently as the pavement weaves through the trees. The tires crunch onto frozen gravel, startling me, and we quickly come to a stop. Ahead, I can make out a wooden observation deck.

Bodie takes my glass and hurls it into the darkness. I hear it shatter against the side of a tree, its destruction soaked up quickly by the cold air. We get out of the car and walk to the platform, which gives us a spectacular view of the city and the lake. He makes some remark about the origins of breaking the glass after a toast but I say nothing. The lights twinkle beneath us. A car is moving slowly across the bridge in the distance but everything else is still.

He leans against the railing and puts his sunglasses back on the top of his head.

"Where else would I have been, Lilith?" he begins, not looking at me but staring down at the city lights."

"Why?"

Bodie says nothing.

I wait.

"He would have discovered his true being eventually. Your attempt on his life just made the discovery more sudden and unexpected."

"He is so calm."

"Of course. He knew but never wanted to fully admit what he is. Only in his writings did he reveal his true self."

"What is he becoming?"

Bodie frowns and turns to me.

"What a ridiculous question. Like all organic creatures, like us, he is in a state of flux. The only thing that is certain is the guardian of death."

"So what is he then?"

"Better," he says, putting his arm around my shoulders. "You want to know. Curiosity is where we come together, you and me. I like it there."

"Me, too," I nod, smiling.

He is staring out over the city again. His voice is as distant as the lake reflecting the city lights.

"He is no accident. He is the product of Amara's sorrow and anger, combined with my expertise and the biological ingredients of his human parents."

"You helped make him? How could you?" I am not angry but I am wary.

"How could I not? I helped Cindy with her creation of humanity. How could I not help Amara in her time of need? Plus I needed to know. I was…curious." He sounds proud of himself but then his voice falters. "But the results…they are…startling. I do not know what he is…exactly."

"What?" My voice is too loud. I slip out from under his arm and stare at him in alarm.

He still will not look at me.

"The only thing I can tell you is he is unique. Everything else I know is what he is not. He is not human. He is not guardian. He is not like anything else in existence. He is…impenetrable…to me."

"So YOU don't know?" I practically shout.

He turns to me. His smile is playful and warm.

"Isn't that cool?"

We both begin to laugh but his is longer than mine. He savours the moment and the irony. I only laugh out of nervousness.

"If it makes you feel better," he adds, with a chuckle.

"Amara doesn't know what he is, either, but she believes he is her Samael, reborn and ready to return to her side. She infused Sam with some of the captured essence of Samael she kept from when you destroyed him."

Bodie will tell me what he will tell me, which is not everything. I do not push him because I can feel his fear like the cold he does not acknowledge on his bare skin, standing on the observation deck dressed for a tropical vacation.

Nothing he says afterwards is of much use to me.

Amara is pleased but surprised about Sam. He is not what she had intended when she helped create him. For the first time, I wonder if Bodie is trying to deceive me. He is frightened of the fury of the forces in motion around him. He wants to be the dispassionate observer, with nothing at stake, just acquiring knowledge, testing hypotheses, not a variable drawn into a deadly equation with an uncertain answer.

I listen as he explains how Amara and her minions located us nearly 50 years ago. Now they follow us easily, even when we change locations and update our disguise. Not only did she not attack immediately, she took great pains to prevent us knowing our façade had been penetrated. I suspected all of this immediately after our attack on Sam had gone awry but I do not stop Bodie from talking. I am waiting for the real intelligence.

He explains how Amara took several discreet steps, herding us eventually to this time and this place, to collide with her secret weapon. Her lack of experience with humans has become evident. She has not considered their stubborn will, their uniqueness. Sam is not simply a pawn but a force onto his own that she has released into our dispute. She is still hopeful, however, that he will prove enough of a distraction for the rest of her plan to come to fruition, ending in our demise.

I finally lose my temper.

"So you have nothing for me, Bodie? Amara knows where we are and has for some time. Her weapon, which you helped create, has not worked as planned. She still wishes to kill me and Cindy. This is not new knowledge to me. Why are you toying with me? You may be the guardian of knowledge but you are not its keeper."

Now Bodie looks at me. He flips his sunglasses back down onto his nose. A smirk crosses his lips.

"Alright, Lilith. I will share my knowledge with you, in a way you will understand better. You have strong feelings for this boy, this creature, but it masks your increasing disdain for humanity. You and Cindy tell yourselves that you enjoy their company but you are increasingly apart from them, which is how Amara found you. You both used to walk with joyful inquisitiveness among humans. Now Cindy is bored of humanity and tired of hiding. You still enjoy humans but only as play things, as toys to amuse you. Sam is nothing to you but an intellectual exercise, a new twist on an old theme. It is not love that blinds you to the threat before you but arrogance. Your enemy is patient and she waits while your lack of respect for her grows. Do you truly understand what she wants?"

I scoff at him.

"Of course I do. I can feel her wants. She wants to kill Cindy for creating humanity and she wants me to die as revenge for taking Samael."

He smiles, nods and pounces on my words.

"And there lies your mistake. She showed you those desires because that is what you expected of her but she hid her true goals from you. Samael's death made him a martyr to her. To avenge him, she seeks to fulfill his dream and eradicate everything."

He steps closer to me. His face is too close, his eyes drill into mine. I cannot hold his stare.

His voice comes slow and soft from his chest but the words are a scalpel.

"But she also wanted you to love her weapon. So now you face the horrible choice she planned for you all along. You will destroy him or he will destroy you and then obliterate all of existence. Either way, she wins."

By the time he is finished, the only place I can look is down. My hands are clasped to my chest, my fingers moving nervously. I finally feel the cold of the night, blowing deep inside. He takes my chin in his hand and jerks my face up to look into his.

"Have I made myself clear?" His freezing hand holds me tight.

"Ya… Yeah… Yes." I gasp. I can hardly breathe.

He runs his hand down my right cheek slowly. I close my eyes.

"You know I adore you, Lilith, but I have always known to keep my distance because you are a snake. Like the reptiles of this world, your blood runs cold and only warms in the presence of heat but you delude yourself into believing the warmth comes from within. You want me to tell you how to destroy Sam but you already have the answer. It is you who toys with me."

He pats my cheek. I squeeze my eyes shut. My hands are now clutching my chest, as if to keep whatever might be inside from falling out.

I can hear the sound of his steps moving away. A car door opens then shuts. The motor hums to life and he is gone.

The heavy sobs make my whole body shake. There are no words to take my pain away. This time, there is no Sam and no comfort.

Reaching out (Sam)

I can't sleep any more.

I'm lying on my bed and I can feel them.

One of them is talking to Lily.

She is receiving information. It tears her apart. I can feel how sad she is.

Mom and Dad also have information I can use.

I need it from them.

Now Lily is walking to me.

She wants me.

That makes me smile.

I want her, too.

Time to move.

Touch (Amara)

"She is even more stubborn than you," Bodie complains, sitting on the steps beside me.

"Oh?" I do not look at him.

"She presumes to know your intentions, just like you do of hers." He has turned to face me, hoping to engage me. I indulge him.

"I presume nothing, Bodie," I turn and stare into his face.

"You know that more than anyone," I purr, patting his knee.

He recoils in shock. When he speaks again, his voice is nervous.

"You touched me."

I am on my feet now and holding a hand down for him to take.

"I know. This human form grows on me. I am appreciating it for the short time it has left with me."

He takes my hand and I pull him to his feet. He looks into my face but I betray nothing to him.

"You are still proceeding." He is not asking a question.

"Of course."

My eyes sparkle and I feel my face smiling again. I do not fight it.

We make our confessions and share our fears (Lily)

By the time I walk down Knox Mountain, through downtown, across Harvey Avenue and into my neighbourhood, the night has faded in the light rising from the east, over the top of Black Mountain. Bodie has left me with much to ponder. My pride tries to convince me he is at least partially wrong but I know his words are truth. The novelty of humanity has worn off. While the species has evolved, our appreciation of their uniqueness has not. Instead, Cindy and I now move among them as leeches, soaking up their desires and lusts. Our tactics will need to change if we are to remain among humans. Sensitive humans are becoming more perceptive of us, increasingly attuned to our presence.

We are becoming more like guardians and less like humans. Our true nature has slowly bubbled to the surface. That is why Amara has been so patient. She has shown a surprising wisdom I had not expected. She knew we could not reject who we are, what we are, indefinitely. She used the pause in the hostilities to refocus, prepare her allies. When we emerge, as she knew we must, she would be prepared, wise to our methods, while we would be hopelessly ignorant of her changes.

Although the weapon has failed, it does not matter whether it worked or not. Its true goal was to flush Cindy and me out into the clearing, where the hunters wait to pounce.

My options are few.

I will have to stay close to the only undetermined factor in Amara's perfect plan. If Sam is a weapon that can hurt Cindy and me, he wields a power that can be turned against any guardian.

The tears are close again but I fight them as I walk. I cannot let the knowledge of what must be done stop me.

There is one thing Bodie is wrong about, I realize. I have no illusions about what I am, what Cindy is, and the lengths I'm prepared to go to preserve our existence. I know there is nothing sincere I can give someone like Sam. He seeks love from me but all I can give him is my yearning for his love. With him, somehow I feel he can alter my nature, make me warm, find the humanity I desire so badly. I know it's not possible but that does not stop me from still wanting it.

I still believe Sam can make it happen. I still hope Sam can save me from myself and in the process I will transform. I will shake this burden and become flesh and blood. I will become real. Why can I not have that? Why can I not make that happen? I want to live a life where living matters, where time matters. I want to love and be loved. I want my heart to beat and I want blood in my veins. And then one day, but not today, I want it to stop.

Suddenly, for a being that has not ever known time except as an abstract, I am keenly aware of how little time remains before my destiny will be decided.

And then I feel his breath, the force of his senses as he reaches out to me.

Even though I'm still several blocks from his home, I can feel him finding me, drawing me to him. I walk past my street and cross over to his, my feet sure of themselves. I feel out of control, his magnetic presence is drawing me to him, yet I am also thrilled. I so desire to be in his orbit, to feel his touch, for him to explore my essence.

His street is quiet and his home is still as I walk on the sidewalk towards it.

Something does not feel right and I glance about nervously. Something is out of place. I am being watched but not in a casual way. Someone is taking aim.

My walk slows as I near Sam's house, my senses sharp. He is near but he is not in the house. Is he being held hostage somehow? Or is he hunting me, ready to fulfill his creator's purpose? Will he attack me here, in so public a place? Every human in the city will hear how a guardian dies.

I want to call for Cindy but I cannot. All I can feel is Sam. He is surrounding me now, gently cradling my closeness. He is calm but he is also euphoric and playful. He is bright and sure and confident.

I stop and close my eyes. If he takes me now, yanking me into that burning darkness inside of him, destroying every aspect of myself, I will not fight. My effect on him is a lie. He has reduced me to standing on a street, willing to embrace my destruction. If this is what it feels like, so perfect and soothing, I will gladly go and leave this place.

There is movement, a soft grunt and the wooshing of air. I am ready now as my time runs out.

On impact, the snowball explodes into millions of icy wet shards, striking my face full on the cheek, just below my left eye.

"Oh, crap," I hear Sam cry and now I can hear the crunch of his boots as he sprints across the frozen ground towards me.

"Lily. LILY!" he shouts. "Are you okay? Oh, god, I'm so sorry."

I open my eyes. I'm smiling as my hand strays to my face and touches the cold imprint the snowball has embedded into my skin.

"Lily, oh, jeez. I'm sorry."

Sam nearly falls on the slippery concrete, stopping so abruptly in front of me. His hand is on my shoulder.

"Are you okay? Did I hit you in the eye? I'm so sorry." His voice is rushed and panicked but its sound is pure tonic to me.

I rush into him and he cannot hold his balance. We fall backwards, landing hard, the thin layer of snow providing no cushion as his back collides with the frozen grass. My hands find his face and turn it to me. My lips hit his temple, his eye, his cheek, his nose and finally find his mouth. I kiss him mercilessly, not letting him catch his breath. He finally begins kissing me back, moving his mouth and tongue. His arms circle me. I feel one of his hands on my shoulder, squeezing it, the other, still cold and wet from the snowball, on the back of my head, stroking my hair, touching my neck.

He tries to break away and speak but I will not let him. I cannot leave the moment. I have found what I want and I will not be denied. Amara and Cindy are gone to me, their concerns and demands burned away. I have found something so perfect and shiny that I can not loosen my grip on it. Time, which just seconds ago seemed in such short supply, is suddenly glorious and endless in this instant.

There is the sound of a door opening.

Sam is now wrestling with me, trying to slip out from underneath me but I am pinning him with my full weight. He is gasping, moving his face away from me.

"You guys, that is so GROSS!" Sara's voice whines high in alarm from the front step. She is already retreating back inside.

"Mom, Sam and Lily are lying on the grass making out. What will the neighbours—" The door closing muffles the rest of her protest.

Sam finally throws me onto my back and jumps to his feet. The front curtain parts and his Dad looks tentatively out of the window, a cup of coffee in his hand and a puzzled look on his face. Still lying on the grass, I wave at him, laughing. He turns away, shaking his head.

I roll over and come to my feet, brushing the snow off my jacket and pants. Sam stands nearby, still stunned.

The door opens again.

"Sam, it's time for breakfast," his mother calls. "Lily, you're welcome to join us, of course."

"I'd love to. Thank you, Mrs. Gardner," I smile at her.

She smiles back and holds the door open. I bound up the steps.

Sam follows slowly.

I am already taking off my jacket and walking down the hall. I hear his mother shut the door behind him.

"Sam Gardner," she whispers, swatting him on the shoulder. "Show some decency and stop molesting this poor girl."

I stop near the end of the hall, at the entrance to the kitchen and dining room. The warm smell of eggs, bacon, toast and coffee greet me. Sam's mom walks past.

"Lily, please come in, sit down." She heads back to the stove to finish the eggs. Sara's back is to me at the counter. I can hear the scraping sound of a buttered knife crossing toasted bread.

I turn back to the hall as Sam comes up to me. "Hey, there, handsome," I smile.

"Hey, yourself," he says, circling me in his arms.

His father walks past us, awkwardly silent. Sam and I laugh quietly together and then follow him into the dining room.

Our meal together is wonderful. We all chat about the holidays and the fine December weather and plans for New Year's Eve. Like the night before, Sam and I are the first up, clearing away the meal, loading the dishwasher, putting away the leftovers and topping up the coffee cups of Sam's parents. Sara has already retreated elsewhere. Sam and I take the last of the coffee, adding hot chocolate mix to make an improvised mocha and we sit down with his mom and dad.

His mom is recalling past Christmases, as a young girl with her brothers and sisters spent on an orchard in Oliver, south of Kelowna near the border.

"What about grandpa?" Sam asks.

A silence descends onto the room. Sam's dad looks into the bottom of his empty coffee cup and tries to take a sip as if there is more of the drink remaining. The head of Sam's mom droops so her chin falls against her chest. She looks suddenly old and burdened.

"Mom?"

"Sam, this isn't really the time," his dad pushes his

chair away from the table and starts to rise to his feet.

Sam's stare at his mother never breaks.

His dad walks over and put his hand on Sam's shoulder. "Please, Sam, another time."

"When?" he asks, sharply. I sit still, trying to make myself invisible.

"We'll talk later," he says, softly. "Tonight."

Sam pushes his chair away and gets up. "Ok, Dad. Tonight. I need to know."

He walks out of the room.

Sam's mom still has not looked up. His dad walks around the table to her. I speak to her before he gets there. I can feel her want for him, for his comfort, to take her away from whatever dark place Sam has intruded upon.

"I'm sorry, Mrs. Gardner. Breakfast was fantastic. Thank you again." I blurt and quickly make my escape.

I chase Sam to his room at the other end of the house. The door is open. He is sitting on the floor, his back against his bed, looking out the window. I have never been here before and I stop at the doorway. I looked at the unmade bed, sheets and blankets in a ball. There is where he stretched his senses, asleep, in his dreams. On the other side of the small room is his desk, where a stack of papers messily covers the top. In those papers, I would find his visions of us, of not just Cindy and me but all of us. He still does not know about the rest of the guardians but I believe he can feel their presence beyond and he is trying to grapple with that knowledge, spewing it from his mind onto paper.

He looks over to me and smiles, patting the carpet beside him. I smile back and sit down next to him, putting my hand on his leg. He puts his arm around me and pulls me close. I rest my head on his shoulder.

"What happened there? That was rude what you did to your mom," I murmur.

He nods, looking out the window again. "I know. I'll apologize later."

He is quiet and I say nothing.

"When mom was talking…about my aunts and uncles…, it reminded me of something…you said last night," he starts again, speaking slowly and tentatively.

I am still and silent against him. His cotton shirt feels smooth against my neck.

"You said…You said I should have…Should have gone crazy or killed myself…by now…for being able to see…To know about you and Cindy…"

I move my head in a slight nod.

"I don't know the details exactly…but I've heard some of the family stories…the history…I don't know what's true…but there's…mental illness in my family… both sides…mom's dad …he did something bad …before he died."

He takes a deep breath.

"And Dad," his voice is stronger now, quicker and more certain. "His mom died in an institution somewhere, when Dad was little."

"You're wondering if Cindy or I had something to do with that."

"Yeah…"

"No, Sam. We didn't."

"Then how—"

"Another of our kind. One who is looking for us. Through your family, I believe she made you what you are."

He takes a deep breath and releases it. "To do what?"

"To kill me, of course."

His body tenses up next to me. "But I thought you couldn't be harmed physically."

"I can't, but you have other means at your disposal."

I know he is thinking about that moment. When Cindy jumped away from him in fear and shock. When I put my hands into him, first to rip his heart away and again to return it. He felt his power. He did not know what it was yet but he knew it was there.

He shakes his head now. "Ok, I need more time. I need to think about this stuff and figure it out."

More time is something I doubt we have much of but I say nothing.

I move away from his arm and face him. "Talk to your father tonight. He has answers to your questions and I know he wants to tell you. When you're ready, call me."

He looks at my face and smiles. "Can I call you like how I called you this morning?"

I chuckle softly in my throat and get up.

"You better."

Distance (Sam)

I lie to her again.

I won't be calling anytime soon and I know that before I shut the door behind her when she leaves for her house.

I don't know who to trust.

Not sure Kathy or Pete can help me here.

"Hey, Kathy. You were right. Lily was hiding something and she ripped my heart out when I found out what it was. No, really, she did. Honest. What should I do?"

Something is after Lily and Cindy.

I have to stay away.

I need to find my own way.

By trying to kill me, Lily showed me that I can be sacrificed, that her and Cindy's survival is more important.

I need to feel some control again.

I want to trust her.

So close (Amara)

I stand outside his window.

It is dark and I am in my human form but I cannot feel the cold.

Steam comes from my mouth and nose, as I take breath as humans do.

He explores me now in his dreams, as he once did her.

His humanity is already fading.

He tells himself he wants answers but what he really seeks is power and control.

He distrusts her.

I stay with him until dawn.

My love.

Heritage (Lily)

Sam does not call that night.

Or the next day.

Or the next week.

The New Year comes and goes.

The return to school approaches and I still have not heard from Sam. Even his dreams have gone quiet to me. Instead of reaching out, it appears his dreams, like his waking hours, have turned inwards. He's not thinking about the rest of the world or Cindy or me. He's examining himself in a mental mirror but his conclusions are invisible to me.

I have to wait.

Pete's mom took the family to Calgary for Christmas to see her parents so Kathy was alone. It was not until the third day of sitting in her basement when she finally asked about Sam. She was shy about it, not wanting to intrude. I sensed she had the same protective desire of Sam that he feels for her. She would not be happy to hear he has been hurt in any way.

I told her an abridged version of the truth. He is spending some time with his family because there seems to be some dark family business, some secret he needs to know about.

"About his grandpa? His mom's dad?" Kathy asked.

"Yeah, that's right," I replied, looking at her curiously.

She met my look but her eyes were distant.

"You know something?" I asked.

She sighed and looks away.

"You should talk to Sam, not me."

"All he told me was his mom's dad did something bad before he died."

She turned back at me with an exasperated look. "I'm sorry, Lily. I want to tell you but it would be best if Sam did, when he's ready."

"He was crazy, right?"

"Lily…" Her look hardened.

"Sorry, Kathy. I just want to help, you know."

We spent a few more afternoons and evenings together, playing board games, looking at magazines, going to the mall, watching TV. Kathy's good nature meant she was quickly able to move on to other things. She was pleased that my curiosity about his family's past is concern strictly for Sam. We talk about Sam and Pete a few times, sharing how we feel we have changed since getting together with them.

This is too personal a topic for me, so I offered little. Kathy sensed my reluctance and kept her distance from discussing Sam.

Now here we are, on the Sunday before we go back to school, walking past the comic book shop in the mall where Sam works. He's inside, taking money from a customer. He is pretending he does not know I am there, watching him, but he has been aware of my proximity from the moment we entered the mall an hour ago.

Kathy walks towards the entrance to the store but I stop her.

"Let's not bother him while he's working," I say.

Kathy stares at me and her eyes widen in sudden understanding.

"Did he break up with you?"

"No, no, I don't think so. I think he just wants a little space, some cooling off time."

"Boys," Kathy shakes her head in disgust. "They want us so bad and then when they get us, they're afraid of losing themselves, losing their identity or independence. Then when you go to talk to them about it, they get all defensive. Like they're the only ones feeling like they're changing into something else."

I smirk and nod. This is what I enjoy so much about Kathy: how right she is even when she does not really know it.

Kathy takes my silence as confirmation of her thesis.

"They say it's getting too serious but it's them getting too serious. They start analyzing everything for some deeper meaning, like they're looking for clues about what it all means. Why can't they just enjoy the moment and let a relationship happen, you know, naturally?"

"If the seed has grown into a nice plant, why worry about how much fertilizer to give it?" I offer.

"Exactly. They get caught up so much about next week that they forget about today."

"Yeah, that's it," I nod with a laugh.

My chuckles quickly change into gasps. I am gulping for air but Kathy does not notice, presuming I am still laughing about her observation. She says something else, gesticulating wildly with her arms, acting something out, but she is not looking at me. My legs are melting beneath me and I wonder if this is what fainting feels like. I shut my eyes but that only makes it worse.

He is coming.

His eyes are on me as he walks out of the store towards us. His focus is solely on me. Instead of the gentle absorption of me that he has done in the past, this is rough and urgent. He is pulling me to him in greedy handfuls, squeezing possessively. I have to concentrate to keep my human form or else he will pull it away. He is pushing to my essence and there is nothing I can do to stop him.

Not that I would try if I could.

The sensation is exhilarating. It is both a warm caress with soft hands and a firm grip of desperate claim. I am being pulled down, my head is going under and I will drown under this wave of ecstasy.

"Miss me?" he purrs, breathing into my ear.

"Yes," I pant, leaning my body into his arms.

Kathy greets Sam enthusiastically but I still can not hear. I am rising to the surface, bobbing and floating now. My faculties are returning to me in splashes of cold water. I think of the snowball Sam threw at me, how it felt against my face. I picture it striking slowly, spreading snow and ice across my cheek as it disintegrated under the impact. The last of the snowball pushes into my skin and there is a puffing sound as the ball of snow surrenders the last of itself, as it ceases being a united ball of snow and completes its destruction.

"Are you on your break?" Kathy asks brightly. "C'mon, let's go to the food court. I want one of those fruit smoothie things."

"Yeah, sure," he says.

He moves beside me and takes my hand.

I squeeze it. Our time apart has evaporated and it now seems the world has resumed its daily revolutions. For the next 15 minutes, Kathy and Sam do most of the talking. Kathy sips her banana drink and chats amiably. Sam eggs her on. I smile, laugh, nod in agreement, snort in derision, whatever I am supposed to do.

When we are walking Sam back to the store, Kathy decides to duck into a shop selling sunglasses, so we can have a moment. We just stand there, facing each other, holding hands, looking into each other's eyes. He is drifting softly through me, gently taking me and cradling me with his senses. Finally, he steps back slowly, letting go of my hands and turns away, walking into the store.

I find Kathy sitting on a bench, five stores away.

"So what did he say?" She jumps to her feet with enthusiasm.

"Nothing," I say, smiling and shaking my head. "Nothing at all."

Kathy opens her mouth, then shuts it, then opens it again. Finally, she just shrugs. "You two. The only thing more confusing than the two of you apart is the two of you together."

We catch a bus home. I get off at Kathy's stop and

thank her for spending so much time with me over the holidays. She just shrugs it off. She is already distracted. Pete is returning home with his family later in the day and she hopes to spend tonight with him, before school resumes tomorrow.

I walk to the house slowly, thinking. Despite our time apart, Sam's hold on me has only deepened. His affection for me is my only hope but it is also the recipe for my demise. If he fulfills his original purpose, I will be powerless to prevent him. Worse, I would welcome him. Knowing this gives me a surprising freedom. I am no longer anxious about the inevitable confrontation with Amara. Sam will either be at my side or hers. Neither outcome seems to matter. Before my essence scatters and the guardian of death bears me away, my last sensation of knowing will be him.

That is enough for me but my surrender has forged a rift between Cindy and me. She has used fury, then logic, then finally last night, she begged me to do something, anything, other than wait for Sam. I explained again what Bodie told me but Cindy countered, stressing how Bodie had said I was incapable of change and I could use Sam to prolong my survival.

Cindy was scared and I tried to comfort her but she would not be calmed. Finally, I was angry with her and called her selfish, blaming her for attracting attention to herself, drawing Amara and others to us. Cindy looked at me with hate in her eyes and silently walked out. I have not seen her since and her presence is far from me.

I will apologize. I am the one being selfish, forcing my way onto her. She has been my companion since the beginning and her loyalty to me is unquestionable. When the time comes, I will respond. Even if I have to die, I will find a way so that she will not be harmed. My hope, which I dare not confess to her because I know she would fight me, is that Sam and I destroy each other. Bodie said I was a snake so I picture in my mind the snake eating its own tail. We will die together, Sam and me, and never be apart.

This will leave Cindy alone to face Amara but I know Cindy will survive. Our inability to find any true allies to stand by us is due to me, not her. I was the one who murdered Samael, not Cindy, and I did so most cruelly. Bodie is not the only one who understands my dangerous nature. Perhaps he is the only one who can put it into words but the other guardians, even humans and the rest of living kind, know instinctively that I am poison in anything but the smallest of doses. Cindy will find her sympathizers. Perhaps she will even make her peace with Amara.

A minivan pulls up alongside the sidewalk and its passenger window comes down.

"Hi, Lily." It is Sam's mother. "Would you like a ride? I have an errand to run and then I'm picking up Sam at the mall."

"Sure, Mrs. Gardner." I open the door and enter the van. "Thanks. I was just with Kathy and heading home."

"Without a hat or gloves in January? I always tell Sam and Sara to dress properly for winter but they never do." She turns up the heat in the van and pulls away.

"So what's your errand?"

"I'm picking something up for Sam from my brother in Lakeview Heights." Her voice shakes slightly. She stares at the road intently, both hands gripping the steering wheel.

"Is everything OK, Mrs. Gardner?" I ask gently.

"Oh, Lily, please. Call me Anna."

"Ok," I say, looking back at the road. She is heading

down Pandosy Avenue towards downtown. The street is busy for a late Sunday afternoon.

It is quiet for a moment except for the clicking of the studded winter tires running over the frozen pavement.

She does not speak until she turns left off Pandosy onto Harvey and is following the flow of traffic towards the bridge.

"Sam's uncle has some things of my father's that Sam wants to see," she says stiffly.

"Oh."

"Remember how Sam asked about his grandpa at Christmas? Well, we don't talk about that much but Sam is curious."

"Ok."

We stop at the red light at Abbott Street. A couple is walking through City Park holding hands. I can see their breath in the cold afternoon air.

"I guess every family has their skeletons in the closet," she says, turning to me. "My Dad tried to kill me when I was pregnant with Sam."

I blink several times, my mouth slightly open. Her eyes return to the road and she starts driving again. I can see the lake grey and somber beneath us as we cross the bridge. Anna is still talking and I am listening and nodding in all of the right places. My thoughts are churning like the water below us.

"I'm sorry."

"Oh, it's alright. It's not a happy story but Sam seems to want to know about it. He's old enough now and it's better that he finds out the whole thing. He's been asking all sorts of questions lately. He asked Art about his mother, too."

"Ok."

"Oh, Lily, I'm sorry. I'm sure you didn't want to get picked up just to hear all of this. Ok, we're almost there. I'll go get this box or whatever it is and then we'll talk about something else on the way back."

Anna pulls up to the curb in front of a large home. The whole neighbourhood overlooks the lake, giant houses squatted on the hillside, huge windows facing the water and the city in the distance. I pretend not to watch as Anna's brother hands her a white cardboard box, the ones used to store office files. He is talking, trying to tell her something, asking her to stay but she scurries down the steps, making a fake apology.

She pulls open the sliding door behind me, drops the box inside, slams the door shut and runs around the back of the van to her door. She jerks the van into gear and pulls away. On the step, her brother stands and stares at us. He looks sad.

Anna keeps her pledge and talks about Sam and his job and the start of school again tomorrow and how she is off work at the bank for another week. Sam is waiting for us at the mall entrance when we arrive. He sees me in the front seat, smiles and jumps in the back seat with the box. He says nothing about it, filling the space in the air by telling his mom about annoying customers.

Unlike earlier, Sam is closed off to me. Even when I reach out to his senses, he remains distant.

"I'll pick you up tomorrow for school," is all he says as his mom drops me off in front of my house.

I thank her for the ride and she drives away with Sam and the mysterious box.

After they turn the corner, I look at our house. It is dark inside. Cindy is nowhere near. I need her now because I am confident she has a good idea about the contents of that box. A few snowflakes begin to fall and the wind picks up. I stare at the approaching storm.

Amara has made her move and I am impressed. I am still not sure my response will meet her challenge but I will face her, with or without Cindy.

Power (Sam)

The thing in me is strong.

I can think about it and start to control it.

I made Lily feel what it was like today, to be subdued and overwhelmed.

I made her feel what I felt like, before I knew what she was.

She loved the sensation, just like I did.

The important thing is I can turn it on and shut it off. She reached out for me in the van and I was able to keep that side of me away from her.

I want more of this thing in me but not yet.

I need to know where I came from.

The box beside me has the answers, I hope.

Mom is pretending it isn't here.

I'm pretending it's not the most valuable thing in the world.

She doesn't look at me as I carry it into the house and head to my room.

Control (Amara)

I consider for a moment going to him in his room as he sorts through the documents in the box.

I am on every page.

My plan, which led to his creation and this moment

of discovery, is in every word he reads and image he sees, yet he still does not perceive me.

His gaze is inward.

"His human ego remains engaged," Bodie says to me as we sit in his car across the street. "Give him more time and he'll see beyond the plan to its architect."

I say nothing in response.

"He doesn't know you yet but he will." He pats my knee in reassurance.

I turn to him. He pulls his hand back in concern.

I lean towards him and he recoils slightly, before he realizes I only mean to give a warning.

"If you don't want to know death right now," I whisper, our faces nearly touching, "you will leave me alone with him."

The sound of Bodie's car has not even disappeared from the winter air and I am already at Samael's window, his lover waiting to be discovered.

Munchausen by proxy syndrome (Lily)

He kisses me gently on the lips the next morning but only his mouth is there. The rest of him, that inner core of him that can sense me and explore me, the part of him I want to touch and be touched with, is closed up tight inside his chest.

"You're testing me," I scold, pulling him close against my body.

He does not resist physically but his voice is as far away as the rest of him.

"I need to understand what I am."

I step away from him and speak to him in my true voice.

"You will not find the answers you seek in that box."

He stiffens. His eyes narrow. "You're right. But maybe I'll find the right questions to ask. I have so many questions for you but first I gotta know these things about my family. And…" He pauses and looks away. "I don't want you to talk to me that way. Not for a while."

I nod. I can't help but smile at him. "Kathy said you'd be like this."

I start walking towards the school and Sam quickly matches my step.

"Like what? What did she say?" His voice is high and indignant.

"It's a boy thing. You analyze your feelings too much, rather than just experiencing them. You worry your feelings will make you lose control."

Sam snorts in his throat and shakes his head.

"Maybe I'm just playing hard to get."

"You weren't playing hard to get yesterday at the mall."

"No," he murmurs. His eyes are seeing things far beyond the end of the street. He takes my hand smoothly in his and we walk in silence to the corner. Students are already hustling inside the school to escape the cold, which has increased dramatically after last night's snowfall. Grey brooding clouds hang close overhead.

Even though the light changes and we can cross the street, he stands still. He clutches my hand tight.

"This is where I first smelled you and I want that again. I want to explore all of that, all of what you are and what I am, whatever that is. I don't want this disguise of you, I want the real thing behind it but I don't want to go in blind because the last time I did, you and Cindy…"

The light turns red again. We'll have to wait. He turns

to me and leans his forehead down so it touches mine. I can feel the warm air coming out of his nostrils against my face. I close my eyes and sigh. It's painful to have him here but not with me.

"If all I can have is the container of you and not what's inside…" I start.

"Ssshhh…" His hand is on the back of my neck.

"But…" I protest.

He puts his finger underneath my chin and pushes up gently. Our eyes meet. "I can't promise I won't hurt you. Until I can, this is what I want."

"Ok." I breathe.

He turns and sees the light has changed back. He takes my hand again and leads me across the street.

"Let's just be like this again, like we were before," he squeezes my hand again.

"Ok."

And it was ok.

I wait for him to tell me what he has found out about his lineage, although I already suspect much of the truth. I wait for Amara to make her move. I wait for Cindy to come back to me. I wait for the inevitable, yet life suddenly moves in slow motion. Hours become days become weeks become months. The seasons change again. Winter loosens its grip on Kelowna. The clouds retreat from the valley and the sun shines warmly, drawing the buds out of the trees in the orchards.

Nothing happens and everything happens. Bodie takes me out for a drive one night and tells me Amara is watching me fall even further in love with Sam and laughing because the betrayal and the pain, when it happens, will be that much worse. She is in no rush because she still believes I will have to murder Sam eventually or he will destroy me—intentionally when I attack him or unintentionally as he explores his power.

"If Amara can wait, I can wait, too," I tell Bodie.

Something is happening, both to Sam and to me. The more Sam finds out about his ancestry and the more he discovers what his abilities, the firmer his grip becomes on insisting to be as ordinarily human as possible.

As for me, I find myself enjoying the humdrum of humanity again. I immerse myself in school and organizing the graduation activities and bringing the yearbook together. Sam's presence always calms me but I discover peace even among my classmates. Their discussions about movies and music and the upcoming weekend start to interest me again. They are so animated, so earnest. I even join in with the gossip from time to time.

I am startled when several people, including one teacher, compliment me on my wit and sense of humour. When I organize a variety show in March, Sam, Kathy and Pete insist I follow the encouragement of the drama club teacher and do a short skit of impersonations of some of the teachers. I privately joke with Sam that living among humans for nearly sixty generations has left me with a detailed knowledge of languages, accents and customs.

Cindy returns to watch the variety show. I feel her laughter over the others in the audience and I realize how much I have missed her. She hugs me backstage afterwards while Kathy and Pete explain in discreet whispers to the curious crowd of students that the ravishing blonde is my mother. While Cindy chats animatedly with Kathy and Pete, Sam slides up to me, congratulates me on a good job and then disappears. He is not ready to be around Cindy and the feeling is mutual. She only fully relaxes once he leaves the building, heading home with his parents.

Afterwards, she takes me out for a fancy coffee and dessert.

"I love the sweetness and richness of chocolate," she coos over her cake, as if she is discovering it for the first time.

Like me, Cindy has used our time apart to reconnect with humanity in the calm before the storm ahead. She flirts shamelessly with the men in the coffee shop and soaks up their appreciative stares.

"I am sorry about what I said, Cindy. We both know it is me who is being selfish."

She laughs and takes a long pull on her straw, savouring the iced coffee.

"You've never apologized to me about anything before now," she smiles. "It seems we are capable of change."

I look down into my empty cup.

"I am not so sure of that."

"Oh, come now. This is not some last hurrah. Can't you feel it? Amara's plan has backfired completely. She sees the love between you and Sam. She's afraid to move against us now because he could turn against her."

"Love?" I stare at her with no expression.

"You heard me," she smiles and meets my stare in return.

She is right, of course. Humans have come and gone in our lives among them but there is a permanence I seek with Sam. By allowing Sam to set the terms for this stage of our relationship, I have put his needs before mine, something I thought myself incapable of, by my very nature. By meeting him on strictly human terms, we have found love. The softness of his cheek, the rough grip of his hands, the deep stare of his eyes, the turn of his smile, the sound of his laugh, the calmness of his voice fills me with more than desire. I want to nurture him and protect him but I also want him to keep bringing these new feelings to the surface.

Somehow, without touching my essence, he is transforming me. I revel in his attention and work to regain his trust.

Sam tells me about the insanity among his grandparents a little at a time. It is April before I have the whole picture. The night I return from Vancouver on a weekend shopping trip for graduation gowns with Cindy and Kathy, he takes me for a walk along Mission Creek and finishes the story.

At the end of January, Sam told me about his dad's mom. Her pregnancy with Art had been particularly difficult and she nearly bled to death after the delivery. She fell into a deep depression and spent her time recovering from the birth in the psychiatric ward. She hardly slept, spending her time on meticulously detailed drawings with an artistic skill she had never demonstrated before. Art's dad burned the pictures after she hung herself a few months later but her sister had secretly kept two of the drawings. Sam's great-aunt would not give him the drawings but let him take pictures. When he showed them to me, I did not see the people in the foreground, torturing themselves and each other with knives and blunt objects, but I stared at the menacing silhouetted shapes off to the sides.

I knew what guardians looked like to a broken human mind. Sam just nodded, chewing his lip in thought, when I told him.

A few weeks later, he told me about the day Anna's

father attacked her during her pregnancy with Sam. As he was choking her, he was crying and told her he loved her but he needed to cut that demon out of her. Art came running in from the other room and they fought. He was cut several times on his hands and arms but he managed to wrestle the knife away from his father-in-law.

Anna's father ran out of the house. Art carried his injured wife to the car to take her to the hospital. Traffic was blocked at Springfield and Pandosy with the lights of ambulances and police cars flashing so he took the side streets. That night, Art and Anna found out the accident at that corner had been her father throwing himself in front of a passing city bus. The trauma from the attack and the news of her father's death was so devastating that she went into premature labour. Sam was born 18 hours later.

Now, with the creek running noisily beside us, its banks starting to swell with the spring runoff from the nearby mountains, Sam tells me what's in the box. His hands are thrust deep into his jacket pockets so I hold onto an arm as the words fall from his mouth. He'll have questions for me and I will answer them as best as I can, even though I know he will be hurt even more by my responses.

As I suspected, what Sam found in the box was himself. The writings of his grandfather are identical to his own frantic words, if not in the actual words then in what they depict. The apocalyptic scenes of human pain, suffering and destruction of the entire species while a malevolent group of angels watches their handiwork unfold with cold detachment. The hopeless, frenzied end to humanity, surrendering itself to its internal madness. There is no room for beauty or love or kindness once their futile existence is revealed to them.

It hurts Sam on so many levels. He questions his sanity. The obvious link between his murderous grandfather and himself frightens him. And a smaller part of him, the writer's ego, is shattered as he realizes there's nothing unique about his words or his vision. Lastly, he blames me and Cindy for bringing all this hurt onto his family.

"Sam, if I could, I would change all of this, I would. I wish you had never met me. You could have lived your life happily without knowing me and Cindy and the rest but I can't. Your family has been pulled into all of this as pawns by others, other guardians who want to kill Cindy and me. I'm sorry for that."

He looks away from me, towards the flowing water.

"You've killed before, haven't you, you and Cindy? Other people like me?"

"Yes, Sam."

"How many?"

"Four—three males and a female."

"Were they pawns, too?"

"We don't know for sure. Probably. A few rare humans seem to have a natural ability to sense us but we suspect they were exposed indirectly to a guardian as a way of keeping track of us and herding us towards your family and towards you."

"To me?"

"What you really are is a weapon, Sam, somehow made by Amara, the guardian of light, with help from someone who I thought was my friend. Anyway, Amara wants Cindy and me gone."

He stops walking.

"That's not all she wants, is it?"

I sigh. I do not want to tell him this but I must not lie. Not anymore.

"She has made you to destroy everything," I mumble, staring into the creek.

"What?"

I face him, grabbing and holding his wrists. I meet his wide and frightened eyes.

"You are dangerous, but not just to Cindy and me. Through your family, you were bred to have the power to—consume all of life itself. And once you reveal yourself to the rest of humanity, your visions, and the visions of your grandfather and the others before him, will be made real."

His forehead wrinkles in disbelief and his mouth turns skeptically. He refuses to believe.

"I was bred to wipe out humanity? Come on. I thought you once told me guardians couldn't have children."

I shrug. "I don't have all the answers, Sam. Art and Anna are your mom and dad but guardians appeared to your family at certain times in the past and it made them more aware of us. And it all led to your birth and then you were…"

I shake my head and look away.

"What?" Sam is impatient.

I look back at him, frustrated.

"I destroyed Amara's lover, Samael. He was the guardian of the dark. I did it to save Cindy when she was being attacked. They would have killed her. Amara kept a part of Samael and I thought she would never let it go but she did."

I squeeze his hands.

"She put it into you."

Sam's head begins to swivel on his neck, turning left and right. His breathing becomes shallow and hurried, his eyes scrambling. He is looking hopelessly for a place to hide from this burden placed on him. He is gasping, choking, and his tears are angry. His mouth and face twist with hurt. Rather than reach out to him with my essence, I know what he needs now. I pull him tight to me. He shakes in my arms. Whatever humanity that I wish was in me, I summon now to help this poor boy, my lovely Sam.

After a few moments, his breathing slows and I feel the calmness return. He sniffs loudly several times and pulls away from me, wiping his eyes roughly with the sleeve of his jacket. In the fading light, his face and eyes are red and inflamed.

"Do you know how to stop this? Stop me?"

I do not hesitate with my answer but my voice cracks saying it.

"Yes."

I blink several times but I am having trouble seeing him clearly through the tears forming in my eyes.

And now he smiles and a quiet laugh forms in his throat. "You can't do it."

The tears burn my cheeks. "No," I moan.

He says nothing. His smile fades to a gentle upturn of his lips. I feel a hot spike of emotion inside me, bubbling to the surface. It bursts.

"I cannot, I will not kill you, you stupid, naïve, innocent, gentle, sweet human, Sam," I scream at him, using my true voice with him for the first time since he asked me to stop. "I will fight to protect you from Amara and all of the others but I would never fight you. I would die, broken by you, and the last thing I would feel is my love for you."

I rush into him, wrapping my arms around him, pushing my burning face into his shoulder.

His arms surround me and his hands fall onto my head

and neck. He strokes my hair.

"So you really love me and you're not just saying that to save yourself?" His voice is quiet and sharp, a perfect gleaming blade.

I squeeze him harder and look up at him.

"I love you, Sam, with all I am. I deserve all the anger and mistrust you have for me. I am not scared anymore. I am not scared of Amara or you hating me or killing me. I just know I love you and that is all I ever want to feel."

He kisses my forehead and I shudder.

I'm a leaf, shaking in a blasting wind.

Knowing (Sam)

Lily's right.

I am the things she says I am.

I can feel it as I stand here holding her. I can feel my human self and then I can feel this other dark part, this separate self.

I have felt Amara watching me for weeks now but I was scared to look back so I pretended I didn't see.

Lily's trembling and crying but I don't know what to think about what she just said about her love for me and not being able to stop me.

Is it all just an act?

Will she use me as her own pawn against Amara?

She seems sincere but I still don't know if I trust her.

Appearing (Amara)

Kyle is polishing his shoes while sitting on the step.

Dan is dancing like a boxer, lightly on the grass, throwing punches in front of him against an invisible opponent.

Nearby, Cherry and Ruby admire their reflections of their human selves in the window to my den. They are wearing matching spring dresses and high heels. They giggle, peering over large, impenetrable plastic sunglasses. They like what they see.

These four were the most devoted of Samael's followers. They were the ones most hurt by his death. I have nurtured their pain and shaped it into rage at Cindy and Lilith.

All four stop what they are doing as I leave the sand and walk up to them. I am carrying my sandals in my hand.

They look at me cautiously, as if I may be angry with them.

"My friends," I hold out my arms and my mouth spreads into a smile. "You have been so loyal and patient. Go to her now. Show no mercy. Leave only the final blow to me."

They run across the sand with joy.

Fading (Lily)

Sam turns the key to start the van as I finish fastening my seatbelt.

"So what is Amara waiting for then? Why haven't she and her friends just attacked you? Why didn't she show herself and come talk to me?"

He puts the van into gear and pulls away. He does not want to look at me and he hides that by driving. I can feel his wariness of me. He knows he is missing parts of the story.

"My friend, Bodie, the guardian of knowing, told me

Amara is waiting because she wants us to be in love. She wants me to have to hurt you or she wants me killed by the one I love. She has been waiting a long time for this so if it takes a little longer, she doesn't care."

"What does Cindy think of all this?"

I smile and turn to him, putting my hand on his arm. I am happy that he does not flinch. I half-expected him to.

"Cindy thinks the whole plan by Amara has gone wrong. She thinks you love me too much and you are too human to do what Amara made you to do. There is too much of Sam and not enough of Samael inside you."

"And what do you think?"

"I like Cindy's theory but I agree with Bodie. Mixing humanity with a guardian has made you into something nobody understands, not you and not even Bodie, but we know you could destroy humans and guardians and everything. Amara is waiting but she is worried about us, me and you."

Sam nods slowly but does not reply. His eyes are facing ahead and his hands turn the steering wheel at the appropriate times but he is not seeing the street or the traffic. I turn away and leave him to his thoughts.

In a few moments, he pulls up against the curb in front of my house. Cindy's SUV is in the driveway and I can feel her inside. After he turns the key off, he takes a breath, deep into his lungs. It goes right past me and into the house. Cindy is startled, her presence now stiff and cold. He breathes out now and I can feel a wave of calmness flow into Cindy. He's issuing his good will, seeking peace with her.

We sit and wait in the quiet of the van for a minute, not looking at each other or saying anything.

The door to the house flies open.

Cindy marches down the steps and across the grass to the van. Using the power windows, Sam slides my window down.

"We need to talk," she says, coldly.

"Ok," I say, undoing my seatbelt.

Cindy looks at me and waves her hand dismissively. "Not you," she spits. "Him. Right now. Inside. Let's go."

She turns and stomps back into the house, leaving the door open.

I turn to tell Sam to be careful and maybe ask if he would like me to go with him anyway. His door slamming in my face is his answer.

"Ok, then," I say, sitting up straight. Sam has even walked around the back of the van to avoid my eyes. He jogs several quick steps, bounds up the stairs and shuts the door before I can say anything through the window.

I get out of the van, close the door and sit on the front bumper. I cannot make out the muffled words but I can hear Cindy shouting. Sam's replies are too low to hear anything. I take anxious glances up and down the street. Thankfully, the weather is cool enough that windows are still closed. It is nearly dark and the street is still.

It is over in less than a minute.

Cindy opens the door.

"Ok, Lily," she says. Her voice has a resignation to it. She does not linger in the doorway so I run across the grass and take the three stairs in one leap.

Inside, the living room is lit. Cindy is just falling back into a chair, sighing. Sam sits on the couch, shoulders slumped with his hands clasped in his lap, looking down into them.

I shut the door quietly behind me.

"Will one of you please tell me what's going on?" I

say, walking up to the coffee table and putting my hands on my hips impatiently.

Neither of them answers.

Finally, Cindy looks up. She glares at me and speaks in clipped tones.

"Sam and I have mended our differences. I have apologized for the attempt on his life. I have also promised to make no further attempts to kill him. In exchange, he has promised to not invade my space ever again."

I stare at her. "I see."

Cindy is used to letting her essence hang about her human form like jewelry. Along with her physical presence, it makes her irresistible to humans. Both men and women chase after her like dogs, lusting after her, forgetting everything else. When it pleases her, she gives them the slightest taste of what she is. For those fortunate enough to experience her, those few moments of physical contact with Cindy burn in their memories for the rest of their lives as if it happened only a moment before.

Sam's senses are beyond such machinations. Even before we knew what he was, his physical response to Cindy annoyed her because it was so muted. His focus was on me, not her, and that was definitely not the way it was supposed to go. Now, it is too much the other way, for Cindy at least. Sam can reach out and sample Cindy's essence as easily as a boy walking through an orchard at harvest time, picking out the fruit at will. There is nothing Cindy can do about it and the loss of control makes her both angry and weak.

On the surface, it appears to him that Cindy is simply demanding her privacy but her request goes so much deeper than that. The reality is Cindy has little willpower to resist Sam's advances on her core. Sam can reach out with his mind, draw her in. If he would keep pulling, he would drag everything in. He could destroy her with little effort and without even the slightest intention.

I take a deep breath and look away from Cindy towards Sam. I have watched carefully as Sam's power has grown recently, hardening like muscle. He can control it consciously, like he just did reaching out to Cindy, but he did nothing to make that power develop. It's growing inside of him, even though he is staying inside his human self.

I can only admire the deviousness of Amara's creation. He wouldn't be able to stop once Cindy and I were gone or once humanity was eradicated. Whether it would be by design or accident, Sam's essence would reach out across the universe, pulling everything inside it with a curious hunger, a black hole, swallowing everything, starting with what was left of his humanity. Nothing, not even guardians, or even Amara herself, could escape. Samael's vision of a perfect darkness for the creator to return to would come to fruition.

All we can hope for is the variable in Amara's equation. Sam's inner strength, his willpower, his self-control, his human self is the only factor beyond her reach. Her disdain for humans makes her not even factor it into her schemes. I find myself smiling, a defiant hope surging inside of me. Amara has no idea what she's dealing with. At Sam's core is a beautiful humanity that cannot be contained by her manipulations. That is what I love. His love for me and for life can save us all.

And there he sits, slumped, a child that has been scolded and is sorry. I feel myself ready to ignite with my feelings for him. He is not the end of existence, he is my Sam that needs to be taken into my arms and reassured.

Cindy gets up and stands beside me.

"Take care of each other, that's all I ask," she says, gently, laying her hand on my arm.

The only sound of her leaving is the SUV growling to life in the driveway.

I sit down beside Sam.

"Are you alright?"

He looks up and relaxes, now that she is gone.

"I didn't know what I was doing, that I was hurting her."

"You weren't hurting her but you could have."

Finally, he turns to look at me.

"That means I could hurt you, too, and I wouldn't even know it."

"I don't think you could that. Not to me." I move my face close to his and touch his cheek.

"How can you be sure?" His forehead is wrinkled with worry.

I move closer, so my lips are nearly touching his.

"Sshhh…Let me show you."

I move quickly to my feet and walk to the wall, flicking the light switch off. With the curtains drawn, it's dark except for the last of the blue daylight filtering into the room.

"Can you see me, Sam?"

"Sorta. The shape of you, I guess."

"Close your eyes. Open them again when you're ready."

"Yeah, sure."

I let my human shape fall away from me. If another human were to enter the room at this time, they might say they saw a ghost or felt the presence of someone dead. They would run to the light switch and flick it on to find nothing there. Most would be terrified and remember this short waking nightmare for the rest of their lives. Others would shed tears over their lost loved ones and go bring flowers to their gravesite and say sorry for not coming more often. A rare few would never be as lucidly sane as they once had been and only the strongest medicines of modern human psychiatry would keep what was left of their minds attached to their bodies.

Sam opens his eyes. I know he can feel me standing there, basking him in what he will later call a perfect soft light but is so much more. I move to him. He is still in human form, breathing lightly. I can feel his heart racing when I take his hand. He pulls me down to him and tries to find my face, to kiss me.

"Don't kiss me with your mouth."

"What? But how—?"

"Like this."

I fall onto the couch and lead him on top of me. I let my fragrance surround him, caress him, draw out what he had seen when he had looked down into his hollow and broken chest the last time he was in this room in the dark.

He is taking me to him in short, sharp breaths but his excitement and his fear of hurting me are combining to hold him back.

"Sam, if you don't let yourself go, you will hurt me. Be calm. Be free. Imagine you're a flower, opening itself up in the morning."

"I love you," he murmurs. He is starting to slip away.

"Your words are of no value here," I say to him with my real voice. "Show me how you feel."

And he does.

The coldness makes me gasp.

I am standing underneath a waterfall, pounded by

the weight and the cold of the water falling from a great height, the roar of the power filling the air. It makes me so awake and aware and alive. I shout in triumph, laughing as I absorb this moment.

I dive beneath the waves and swim across the dark pool in wonder and then rise to the surface, panting in delight, my face coming out of the cold water and into the warm sun of him. His heat and his light on my face are caressing me. I run out of the pool and fall to the grass, giggles fluttering like butterflies out of my throat.

I shiver. It is spring and the air is cold on me, making my skin taut. His sun shines on me and I open my eyes, my arms, my legs to it, surrendering myself to his energy.

When there is nothing but him, nothing but the light and the sound of rushing water, I reach up and grab the sun, nestling it in my hands like a fragile crystal. And when I look inside of it, I see him there, tiny and reflecting back to me a million ways, kneeling in the sand on the shore of a perfect beach at night, staring into the moon shining in his hands.

He looks up at me and a dangerous wind blows through me, shaking the trees, startling the grass. Now I look up and I see his soft eyes, as huge as the sky, gazing down at me, inside the sun.

I can only stare back, unable to breath, unable to move, so tiny and so safe under his watchful gaze. This is where forever is. I am laughing and crying now but I still cannot look away. In those eyes I see his love for me as salvation, a symbol of hope that makes sense of all of my empty wanderings across billions of years and the width and breadth and depth of the whole universe.

And then he blinks and looks away.

I fall to the ground, screaming. The rocks are sharp

and hot, cutting me. The wind whips me and no matter which way I turn, it cuts into me, leaving deep gashes that spray blood. There's a hand on my face, crushing it. I cannot breathe. What is happening? What is he doing?

"Lilith."

I cannot move my head to find the voice. It is not his voice. It is a woman's voice and it is urgent.

"Lilith," it calls more urgently.

Cindy?

I strain and squirm but I am trapped. I feel sharp blows fall on me from all directions, breaking my bones. I can feel them on her, their teeth sharp as predators. I was so distracted I did not even recognize Cindy's voice until it was too late.

Now Cindy's voice is screaming my name.

I look to the sky and see black angry clouds cover the sun and then rain falls on me like acid. I gasp and I leave this place, where I was with Sam, where we shared this moment, so perfect. He has already departed. He felt what was happening before I did.

My human form is still taking shape around me in the dark as I see Sam throw open the door and run outside.

"No, no, no," he's moaning loudly.

Barely able to move, I stumble and follow him. Still half-blind, I collide with him on the top step. He's looking at the sky, which is not black but filled with bursts of light. There are deafening crashing sounds.

Inside the bursts of light, I see what they are doing to her. With each blow, I feel a whip across my back. I am powerless to stop what is happening. There are strange sounds coming from my throat. I recognize them as whimpering. The tears cloud my eyes.

"Amara…" I whisper. "Amara…please…I beg you…

Please don't."

The only reply I hear is Cindy.

She says my name one last time. It comes to me quietly but the sound of it is rough and forced and rushed.

It is the sound of someone leaving.

Then a clear, hideous snap.

A terrible silence follows and the sky is black again.

Sam is pulling me back in the house, slamming the door behind us.

I fall to the floor, hitting my head hard against the corner of the wall. He kneels over me in a protective crouch.

A huge gust of wind shakes the house, making it groan as it strains to hold itself together.

Then it is gone and Sam is sobbing violently but I am numb.

I lie here in a coma, my eyes opened and unfocused.

Equilibrium (Amara)

I take no joy in the act.

I hear Lilith's plea but I do not reply.

I say nothing at all, just like she did to me.

Unlike the others, who celebrate their victory, I do what I have to do.

It is what Samael wanted.

Alone, I return to my cabin on the beach.

I wonder if Bodie will be on the steps waiting but he is not.

He is with him now.

As it should be.

Eulogy (Lily)

I felt Cindy die.

Cindy knew humans so much better than me and I trusted her guidance.

I know their secret desires, their fiercest yearnings, but Cindy knew what made them live and thrive.

She bathed in their lust for life and creation because it was the truest reflection of her essence.

With them, with me at her side, she felt perfect.

She finished what I began.

New desires began as she fulfilled others.

We nourished each other.

I knew she was there and her value to me but I did not know her.

Cindy was the place I could point to but never go.

Cindy was the sanctuary I could lead everyone to but never know the way.

Cindy was the fruit I could grow but never pick.

Without her, there is no harbour but only the false hope of one.

Without her, there is no completion, no satisfaction, no culmination.

Before I could ever be alone, before I had any time to consider, Cindy was there.

She sprang from the burst of creation straight into my arms.

We laughed together and danced in the newness of existence.

The answer to the question I never asked.

The water for the thirst I would never quench.

The food for the hunger I would never satisfy.

Wide awake (Sam)

I'm still crouched over Lily, long after I stop bawling

my face off.

I hold her close but I'm the one who needs the holding. I felt Cindy die and it felt like drowning. There was no air and a short fight.

I was the bait. Lily had been with me and left Cindy alone. Amara made her move.

I am not sure why Amara isn't here right now to finish the job. I doubt huddling over Lily will protect her even if Amara does come but I can't think of anything else to do.

Lily's gone anyway. I hold her body but she's nowhere in sight. I hope she has the strength to come back to it. Come back to me.

That makes me cry some more.

There's a sharp knock at the door that startles me but I don't move. My eyes are wide and, in the quiet, I can hear my heart beating anxiously. There's only silence after that huge wind that marked Cindy's passing. It's too dark. There's no light from the street. I think the power has been knocked out by the storm.

Another knock, this one softer.

The door opens slowly and then quietly closes.

I wait for the worst.

Instead, a gentle hand on my shoulder.

"Sam, my name is Bodie. I am an acquaintance of Lily's. You have nothing to fear from me and neither of you are in any immediate danger. I am here to help."

I feel a sharp gasp from him as I let my awareness reach out to him. He squeezes my shoulder tighter but says nothing.

I know he's telling the truth. I see he knows much more than that but I don't care right now.

"Ok," I say, straightening up, staying on my knees, my hand on Lily's head. I don't look at him yet. "What do we do?"

"You have human responsibilities that require your attention," he says, crouching down on one knee beside me. "The storm has knocked out the electricity to much of the community. You did not return for the evening meal and your parents have been unable to locate you. Your father is on his way here now. You must leave."

"No, I can't," I nearly shout. "Not now."

"You used your power to learn I mean no harm and my words are true. I will tend to Lily and there are other arrangements that must be made in the wake of Cindy's death. We will talk again before you attend school in the morning and I will explain more."

"But—"

"Now, Sam." He grips my arm. "Your father approaches. He must not see Lily like this. She cannot be seen by human eyes."

I scramble to my feet and look down at Lily but I can barely make her out in the dark. If the lights in the room came on, I have a hunch what she would look like. She's fuzzy and unfocused, not quite tuned in to the proper frequency.

And then a shock in my head, there and gone as fast as the flash from a camera. Dad's concern. He's coming up the sidewalk with a flashlight in his hand. He's three houses away.

I feel him.

"Ok, Bodie," I say, still staring at Lily lying defenseless on the floor. "I need to know what's happening. Find me later."

It feels so wrong but I walk out of the house, closing the door behind me and trying to get my normal face on. I hope I don't look like I've been crying.

I turn and concentrate on the bobbing beam of light approaching.

"Dad? Is that you?" My voice sounds steady, almost normal.

On the way home, I make up some story about how Lily just fell asleep while waiting for Cindy. He scolds me for not coming home but his heart isn't in it. I can hear the relief in his voice.

It smells like a gift shop in the house when we get home. Mom has lit every scented candle she owns and placed them around the kitchen and living room.

Being around Mom calms me. Her worry about the power and how many trees have been knocked down by the wind storm and the fish in their tank in the living room and her fussing around the house and fussing around me is a nice distraction. I can pretend to be normal and fully human, even if I don't feel that way inside.

I'm just starting to understand I'm different, that Mom and Dad inadvertently made something dangerous when they had me. I can't carry all of that in my head for very long. So as Sara glares at me for cozying up to Mom, I felt better even being near her spite. It's real and I need some real right now. There'll be time enough later for the unreal or the more than real.

I gobble up the two ham sandwiches Mom made for me. She watches with approval as I also eat a banana and drink two big glasses of milk. At least I'm still normal there. I'm hungry all the time and my full stomach helps me also swallow what happened earlier. I'm in shock but Mom and Dad are just happy to have their boy back. I try to stay in the moment for them because I can't be sure there'll be many more times like this ever again.

After a huge yawn, Mom scolds me to my room. I

don't realize how exhausted I am until I fall onto my bed. I'm thinking I should get undressed and get under the blankets but sleep catches me before I can do anything else. The next time I open my eyes, my clock radio numbers are flashing red. The power is back. The house is quiet. It's still dark out but it's grey. The new day is coming.

I don't move. I can hear a car idling softly in the street and know Bodie is waiting outside for me.

Something else is out there, too.

Two of them. I can feel them.

Is this a trap? What's going on?

I jump to my feet, my fists clenched. I don't care what happens now. If they can kill Cindy and do whatever they did to Lily, what chance do I have?

I let myself quietly out the window, stepping into the hedges. I brush off the shrubbery cling-ons as I walk across the lawn to the old convertible sitting at the curb. It's mild out but it's still too chilly to be without a jacket so I pretend not to feel the cold. I ignore Bodie, sitting in the front seat with the top down and wearing a loose muscle shirt.

In the back seat are two girls, a couple of years younger than me, who must be twins. They are wearing matching summer dresses, like they are going to some formal event with wine and rich people at someone's mansion on the lakeshore. They are thin and their hair is perfect. They are staring at me but I can't see their eyes through the huge sunglasses that cover the top half of their faces. They are smiling at me but seeing their teeth just makes me shiver.

"Sam, may I introduce Cherry and Ruby?"

"Hello," they chime together, giggling.

"Uh…hi."

"I've got coffee, Sam. Get in," Bodie says, snapping me out of the staring contest with the two girls.

He smiles at me as I get into the car. He hands me a steaming coffee and just cradling the hot take-out cup in my hands warms me up.

"Who are they?" I whisper as I take the cup, leaning towards Bodie.

"Hey, we're right here, Sam. We can hear you" says one of them, startling me. They are both leaning forward, resting their upper arms on the back of the seat, their faces close.

Bodie puts the car into gear and silently pulls away, refusing to look at me or answer my question.

"We're friends of Amara's," says the one directly behind me. Their voices are as identical as their appearance. They take turns talking.

"We trapped Cindy last night…"

"…and then Amara got rid of her."

They both giggle at that. The sound of their laugh is warm.

"What are you doing here?" I say as cold as I can, refusing to look back at them, hoping I sound brave because I don't feel it.

"We wanted to meet you."

"Just to say hi."

"We'll be at your school today."

"Just to keep an eye on you."

Bodie turns the car down Lily's street.

"We're here to watch her, too."

"Just in case."

He parks in front of the house and turns the car off.

"She's not conscious yet and will not be for some

time, if ever," he says.

I look at the house and reach out to her with my mind. I spill the coffee on the floor as I scramble to open the door. I finally get it open but then trip, falling out, scraping my knee on the pavement. If I could crawl under the car, I would. I feel this overwhelming need to hide but I know there's no place those eyes can't see.

I stay there in the driveway, on my hands and knees by the car, squeezing my eyes shut. I know if I look up all I will be able to see are those eyes, everywhere, staring eyes watching me, assessing me, endless pairs of eyes in the air and the sky, following my every move. I can feel Cherry and Ruby as they stare at me. I feel myself melting away under the heat of their gaze. They don't blink. They just stare.

Bodie's hand is on my shoulder again. I can hear the giggling in the back seat of the car. One of them accidentally snorts, which leads to even more chuckles.

"I would rely strictly on your human perceptions for the next while, Sam," Bodie says gently. "Cherry and Ruby are watching your every move. They do not share Amara's confidence in you and so you remain under their constant surveillance."

I shake my head and take a deep breath, trying to swallow. I push those eyes to the side but I can still feel them there, like an extra weight hanging over me. Bodie is encouraging me back into the car.

"We told you we had our eyes on you."

"Just so you aren't mad."

I push their voices to the same place as the eyes, off to the side. I hear them but I don't want to listen.

"Sorry about spilling the coffee," I say to Bodie as he climbs back into the driver's seat.

"Did you burn yourself?"

"No, I don't think so," I lie. I can feel my skin hot under my jeans where the coffee has soaked through.

Bodie smiles at me.

"You may attempt to deceive me about that but I would appreciate you not lying to me about any of the other more pressing matters we are here to discuss."

His smile is even bigger now, cool and intelligent. If he was dressed in a high school principal suit, I would have instinctively answered "yes, sir, sorry sir." Now I can just look down at the wet coffee stains on my pants and nod like a scolded preschooler.

"I have put some matters into motion in the human world. After receiving a tip from an observant citizen out walking his dog later this morning, the police will discover Cindy's vehicle at the bottom of a canyon. It will appear to them that she was driving too fast and missed the corner. Inside, they will discover her body. It is not her body, of course, but it will be enough to satisfy the investigators."

I can't look up yet. I just keep nodding, stupid and quiet.

"By midday, a male police constable, two women representing victim services, and a man from a government agency for child welfare will arrive at this house. I will tell them that I am Lily's father and I was called here by Lily when her mother did not return safely last night. Their records will indicate that I am, indeed, her biological father. I will not let them see her as I will demand our privacy and ask that I be the one to inform my daughter about her mother's death. Once they leave, I will make the other death arrangements to satisfy human custom in this country."

"Ok," I sigh.

"You will attend school as normal. I will call the principal in the morning to inform him that Cindy is missing and then again when we receive the news about her death. He will take you aside and tell you what he knows. You must act distraught. You may come here for a short time this afternoon and then you will go home and tell your family."

"Yeah, sure."

"We have a few moments, Sam, before I must return you home. Do you have any questions for me at this time?"

I grunt.

"Only about a million but I can't ask most of them with those two here," I say, looking at his face, which is blank as a poker player's. "How about I ask the obvious first—why are you here?"

Except for a little turn of his mouth, his face doesn't change.

"You do not know?" He's looking at me like I'm a curious coloured bug on the road. It's hard to tell whether he's asking a question or making a statement of disbelief.

"You're one of Lily's friends, I guess, and you're here to protect her and fight Amara if she comes," I blurt out hopefully.

Below the stream of giggles that erupt from the back seat is Bodie's laugh, which comes from down low and flows thick from his throat. He won't stop staring at me, even as he laughs. I reach for the door handle. It'll only take me a minute to walk home and get away from this jerk and these two annoying girls.

"Sam, I am sorry for laughing at you," he says but he's still not finished having his big yuk at my expense.

"Please forgive me."

He starts the car and is moving before I can make my getaway.

"I am not here for Lily because she is not looking for me. I came here at your request, whether you know you called for me or not. I am here to explain some issues of concern to you. Serving as Lily's father during this time simply allows me to be in your proximity without attracting undue human attention to myself. You seek knowledge and this is my field of expertise. Do you understand?"

This isn't what I expected. I sit there, chewing my lip, trying to take in what he just said. I summoned a guardian? How did I do that? Lily's still alone to face Amara. My head is filling with more questions.

We pull up across the street from my house. He puts the car in park but leaves it running.

"As I told Lily when she came to see me, you are the first creature I have ever encountered that I cannot penetrate so I do not know what you know and what you do not know, although I can deduce some of it. I will try to give you some of the answers you seek but you must be patient because my answers will also give you more questions. Some questions you will either have to ask Lily or find explanations on your own."

"But what about—?"

"You must go now. Your father stirs in his bed. Play your part today at school and then come see me this afternoon at the house. We will talk more."

There's no getting past that old, blank face of his. If he can't work his way into me, I know the opposite isn't true. I can push my awareness into him and take everything he knows. He won't be able to stop me.

He looks into my face carefully, as if he's studying a

distant galaxy through a telescope.

"Knowledge comes with a cost, Sam," he says, not breaking his stare. "I know enough about human nature to know what you are considering. At school today, please reeducate yourself about Pandora's jar. Like all myths, it is steeped deeply in truth. I am that jar and you, at this moment, are Pandora, the all-gifted. You are in a danger-ous position. If you value what you are, you will make your next choices carefully."

"You mean Pandora's box, right?" I ask, smirking.

"No, Sam. I mean jar," he answers slowly. "I was there."

I look down and nod. Bodie seems to have that effect on me.

"Now go," he orders.

"Bye, Sam." The chorus from the back seat calls out.

I get out of the car and don't wave goodbye.

I reach my window and push my way through the hedges and inside. The car is already gone as I slip the window back down.

Loss (Amara)

I try swimming but the foreign experience of water does not wash away how I feel, no matter how long I let the wetness soak me.

I am sad for Lilith and, for the first time, I consider the wisdom of my plan.

Samael ordered Cindy's death to bring Lilith into line and to eliminate the spark that forged the creation of life and of humanity.

He did not consider the cruelty of it.

Lilith made me experience this brutality and now I

have made her experience the depth of my malice in return. I should feel avenged but instead I feel as empty as the moment Samael was taken from me. I know what she is experiencing now as no other does. Even though I knew taking Cindy away from Lilith would not bring back Samael to me, I still acted.

I already have brought Samael back and soon he will be at my side, despite the lack of faith of my loyal supporters. Except to make them happy, I did not need to remove Cindy, as she was no obstacle to my plans.

Now I fear for myself.

I have become like Lilith.

I took the life of another guardian not because it needed to be done but because I could, because I had the power and the will to do it.

I try to lie on my back and float in place but my thoughts weigh me down and I keep sinking beneath the surface.

Love (Lily)

In the moment I found love, I lost Cindy.

Sam heard her pleas for help even before I did.

I was too busy discovering myself, rejoicing in the love I found for Sam and he found for me.

Maybe this was the way it had to be.

Could I not find love and keep Cindy as well?

By forging one beautiful new link, was I severing another?

In the moment I could see the end of myself, she was taken from me.

In the moment I saw the doorway to another existence, past my endless yearning, a door Sam held open and smiled and held out his hand and was ready to take me through it, to where Cindy was, to where all my unsatisfied desires could be made whole, to where I could lose myself and become whole all at once, she was denied to me.

We were denied to each other.

Severed (Sam)

"Where's Lily?" Kathy asks as I open my locker.

I practised this moment in my head all the way here and I still don't feel ready. Little white lies always come easily to me but big whoppers like this are much harder. I know I won't be able to keep a straight face. But what can I say?

Lily and I were sharing something way more intimate than sex (because Lily's not human and I'm still human, I think, but not like everybody else) when some force that goes by the name of Amara and is the cosmic representation of light attacked Cindy (who is also a cosmic representation of something that combines creativity and sex and passion all into one) and destroyed her.

And now there are two new students in Grade 10 that everybody's talking about because they're identical twins named Cherry and Ruby who are cute and wonderful, except that they're guardians here to spy on me or just torment me, I don't know.

On my way to school, when I should have been thinking about my story and what I needed to say and do at school today to protect Cindy's and Lily's (and Bodie's) identities, I couldn't stop thinking about that moment with Lily. What do you say about an experience where you melt into someone and they melt into you, literally, body and mind? There's nothing left to say when you don't have to say 'I love you,' when you can just open yourself up and show it. I experienced Lily's love.

I looked at the mirror this morning, before heading down to breakfast, and I still looked the same—the same geek with the unruly hair and dopey eyes and skin made from the before-segment of an acne medication commercial. Yet I felt disconnected from my body, like my skin and bones were an anchor holding me from a place where I could be with Lily always.

The air and the sun didn't feel right on the way to school. I took a different way, rather than walk past Lily's house. I knew I wouldn't be able to stop from reaching out to her and I wasn't ready to face those eyes again. I had driven Cherry and Ruby back far enough in my head to just a nagging sense that someone was watching me from around the corner. Yet in the school halls, it seemed like I could hear them all the time. I wouldn't be able to live with this feeling, this low-grade paranoia, for long. I had to find a way to look back.

Everything's happening too fast. I need time to wrap my head around Lily's love for me because I'm still not sure how a girl older than creation falls in love for some high school guy from Kelowna. I like to think I'm special but I know how hopelessly ordinary I am, too. Well, at least my human part is ordinary; I've had some stuff from this Samael guardian put into me so I guess I'm not ordinary. Hey, you're starting to get it. It's not ordinary for guys to see guardians or be able to kill everyone just by thinking about it and wipe out the universe.

I need time with Bodie to help me understand what happened with Cindy and what all this stuff with Amara and the rest of the guardians is about. This isn't a fight between two girls over hurt feelings. This is war between people (or creatures or beings or guardians or whatever) who have the power to kill all of the human race, shape the universe and who knows what else. How did they kill Cindy, anyway?

"Hey, Sam, come in, Sam. It's Kathy calling. Can Sam come out to play?"

Before I have to answer Kathy and face everything ahead of me, I still have to be Sam. Thinking about Kathy standing behind me, too sweet to have an irritated look on her face when she should really be ticked, makes it easy to be the Sam she knows.

I turn around and look at her face.

What took Pete so long? She's gorgeous and not just the freckles around her pale face and those beaming blue eyes and that burning red hair. She's spilling over with gentleness and caring and sincerity. There's no way I can lie to her but no way I can tell the truth, either.

Where's Lily, she asked. That's so hard to answer. I look away.

"She's at home," I say, flat and quiet. "Cindy didn't come home last night and she's not answering her cell."

"Oh, God," Kathy gasps.

Now her arms are around me, her hands pressing into my back. Her hair smells like lilacs.

She lets me go but her face is close.

"Has she called the police? Does she have anyone to help her? Is she alone?" Her voice is fast and rising in panic.

Before I can answer, Pete shows up, complaining about the hug he saw from down the hall. Kathy shuts him down with her worry about Lily and Cindy. He looks at me with concern mixed with a hefty shot of annoyance.

"Buddy, why are you here?" I can hear the scorn. "Your girl needs you."

Because Bodie, the guardian of knowledge, told me to be here.

Because "my girl" is in something like a coma, except no doctor in this world could explain why a teenage girl could look like she was not completely there, at least in a physical sense, like the fuzzy projection of a person instead of the real thing.

Because I don't think the macho I'll-protect-you-baby thing is what "my girl" needs right now.

"Her dad is there."

"What dad? I thought Lily said there was no dad around," Kathy asks.

"Well, when I went there this morning, this guy who said he was her dad but looked old enough to be her grandpa was with her and they were waiting for Cindy or the police to call."

Bodie has given me an easy cover story. I can completely tell the truth but the whole thing is a lie.

Pete is still giving me that look that I'm not fulfilling my masculine chivalry duty but the bell rings for first class.

"She'll call when she finds out what's going on, right?" Kathy's hand is on my arm.

"Yeah, sure."

I head off to geography, grateful to leave them behind me so they won't see my slight smile. It isn't just that they bought my story but that they are so Pete and so Kathy. They're my friends and they care about me and about Lily, too. I may be alone with all this other crap over my head but in my Sam space, they're here for me and that feels good.

In class, I pay attention more than usual. I listen and take part in a discussion about the ongoing problems with resource scarcity in Africa and how that has a direct connection to oppression, war and genocide. During break, I hurry to my law class, sitting alone at a desk and avoiding the crowded hallway. My schedule doesn't include Kathy or Pete until the afternoon biology class with Kathy so I want to steer clear of them until at least lunch time. Pretending to be someone else is fine with teachers but I want to avoid having to do it with my friends as much as possible.

Kathy is waiting for me at my locker at the start of lunch period.

"Pete will be here in a minute. Drop off your stuff and we'll walk over to see Lily," Kathy instructs me in her soft but firm tone.

Bodie didn't take my friends into consideration when he came up with this plan. I slowly put my books in my locker, trying to figure out how to wiggle out of this jam. It only takes 10 minutes to walk to Lily's house, which leaves us 20 minutes there before we have to walk back so we won't be late for our afternoon classes. Pete jogs up to us just as I'm closing the locker.

"Okay, let's go," he says, urging us down the hall toward the main doors.

"Yeah, sure."

I don't know what to do or say so I just follow along, trying to keep up. My brain is too crammed with everything else to come up with some excuse for not going to see Lily. My only hope is Bodie will be at the house and will tell them she's sleeping and they are still waiting for news. That would be a pretty lame story and I wondered if Kathy or Pete would even fall for it.

As we march through the doors and head for the street, I consider trying to reach out to Bodie with my mind. I know I can do it but what about Ruby and Cherry? Will they stop me?

"Hey, who's that?" Pete asks, slowing down.

Principal Atkinson, dressed in an expensive suit, crisp white shirt and shiny bright tie as usual, is chatting with a tall, skinny scruffy guy with oily greyish hair that hangs flat and limp to his shoulders. The principal's professional clothes make Bodie's beach shorts, grubby muscle shirt and flip flops seem even more tattered. He looks like a guy who has spent too much time camping out on a beach in Mexico with an old guitar and a bag of dope.

"That's Lily's dad," I say, stopping.

"What?" Kathy says, a sharpness in her voice I've rarely heard before.

"You've got to be kidding me," Pete says, a sharpness in his voice I know very well. "That old geezer… and Cindy…"

I can't help but let out a low laugh. I hadn't thought through that part of Bodie's story and how it would look to people when he came around saying he was Lily's dad. Not only did he not look like his "daughter" at all, anyone who knew Cindy would find the idea of someone like him getting within five miles of someone like Cindy to be pretty weird.

Bodie sees me and waves casually, a flick of his hand that barely goes higher than his hip, as he continues explaining something to Principal Atkinson.

I take this as an invitation to walk over to them. Kathy and Pete trail a few steps behind.

"…would most appreciate your discretion during this sensitive time," Bodie finishes as I step up to them.

He turns from Principal Atkinson to me and puts a hand on my shoulder.

"Sam, I have some bad news about Lily's mother." His voice is mild and formal in a professor sort of way. It's the sound of authority. Despite his appearance, I know anyone who hears what he has to say in his human form will stop in their tracks to listen. "Cindy's body was found in her car at the bottom of a canyon about an hour ago."

I wondered how I would handle this situation when it arrived. Now, standing here, with Principal Atkinson looking at me in concern, and hearing the gasp of shock from Kathy behind me, I don't have to fake anything. Bodie's hand on my shoulder reminds me of when he put his hand on my shoulder last night, in the dark, huddled over Lily. In his eyes is the full knowledge of Cindy's death and what it means to Lily and to me.

"Oh, no…no," my mouth is moaning softly.

I'm with Lily again, in that perfect moment with her, connected and vulnerable, when I felt them attack Cindy. It was just a tug at first, an annoying distraction from the wonderfulness of Lily, but then it was a sharp pulling, a yanking, away from Lily. In that second, before I returned to my Sam self, I could feel what they were doing to her. Now I know how they did it. To destroy her, Amara, Cherry, Ruby and the other guardians ripped her to pieces.

I'm blinking fast now and my sight gets blurry as I start crying.

I'm running to the door again, begging them to stop hurting her but knowing they won't. I feel Lily stumble into me as I looked into the sky and saw, with human eyes, what it looked like when a guardian died. And then that sound, which everyone thought must be thunder. It was the sound of being torn, of something that had been connected to Lily and the rest of the universe since the beginning of time being cut away. It was a tree that had been standing for centuries being chopped down with one terrible swing.

Bodie takes his hand away and turns back to the principal.

"Lily would like to see Sam. She is alone at the house right now and I do not want her to be by herself for long."

"Of course, of course," Principal Atkinson springs into action. "Sam, you're excused from class. Please give Lily my sympathy."

Bodie is already walking towards his old convertible, parked at the curb.

I turn to Kathy and Pete but can't look at either of them except for a short, cruel glimpse. Kathy's face is wet and she looks like she's been beaten. I can't look at her eyes because they feel so sorry for me and for Lily. Pete stands there stunned and lost. They both look like how I feel. Seeing my friends like this just hurts more.

"I'll call you later," I choke out, scrambling away to catch up to Bodie.

Getting into the car and pulling away happens in a fog but the breeze on my face clears my thoughts. I wipe my eyes and turn to Bodie. His face is grim and his mouth is turned down.

"Sam, Lily continues to fade from existence and another guardian approaches."

"What? Amara?" I shout, sitting up straight.

"No, not Amara. This guardian has no name and no shape to us but you would call her death. She is where Cindy went last night and now she considers Lily. She is close by and she waits for Lily to decide."

"Decide? Decide what?" I demand as Bodie takes the

corner smooth and tight. The house is in sight.

"Whether she wants to live or die."

Surrounding the house are the eyes of Cherry and Ruby. They see me and they are bright with laughter.

Killing (Lily)

Cindy did not fight when Amara came.

In her separation from me, Cindy reached out to the guardian she knew would take her.

Is this what Amara felt?

Is this what she experienced when I took Samael from her?

We are sisters, Amara and I, limitless in our cruelty.

I could never stop feeling her desire for my death but in that desire, she hid her true wants.

She wanted me to suffer. I see that now.

She wanted me to know what it was like to lose the half of yourself that gives you meaning.

For the first time, I see myself, a sharp edge at the end of a bloody knife.

I see what I have cost others.

I see what I have cost myself.

Little girl (Sam)

Bodie hasn't stopped the car in the driveway yet and I already have the door open to get out. Thankfully, the front door is unlocked so I rush inside. I'm breathing heavily as Bodie follows a second later, closing the door quietly behind me.

The house is still and quiet. Without saying a word, Bodie motions with an arm out to the hallway. I head for the far bedroom where Lily lies on top of the bed. The first time I was here, I had been amazed at all of its treasures, the souvenirs from all the lifetimes spent among humans. Art hangs everywhere on the walls. The ornate curtains are partially closed but they still let in the light.

I step inside the room but stop by the door. Bodie walks past me and up to Lily, looking down at her closely. I open my mouth to ask him about the other person in the room but then I make eye contact with her and decide against it. Bodie doesn't seem to see the little girl in the far corner.

She looks like she's six or seven years old. She's wearing a blue summer dress with sparkling black shoes, like she's going to church. Her brown hair is neatly combed and pinned back to fall past her shoulder. In one hand, she holds a string attached to a red balloon that floats gently in the air above her. In the other hand, she holds a bouquet of yellow and white flowers. She's going to a funeral.

She wears the gentle innocent face and bright eyes of a kid but I know who this little girl is. Bodie said death has no shape to guardians like him but I'm still human and I know death when I see her. I'm not scared at all. No one can be afraid of where someone this adorable will lead you.

She looks at me expectantly, studying me. Then she looks at Lily and her face darkens. My eyes follow and I take a sharp breath. Lily is nearly gone. I remember a word from a high school English class. Translucent. I can still see her but I can see through her. Her shape is here but she's not solid. Her eyes are closed and her face is calm but she's not here.

I walk to the foot of the bed and Bodie looks at me.

"I need you to leave the room," I say, meeting his

eyes.

Bodie raises an eyebrow and then looks down at Lily, forming his lips into a grin.

"I know what you're planning," he says, nodding in approval. "You are going to search for her in the void."

"Then you also know that I can't do that with an audience," I replies.

He looks back at me.

"Cherry and Ruby are still watching."

"I know but I don't think they'll follow where I'm going."

He nods again but says nothing. Finally, he walks to me, putting that hand on my shoulder again. I don't look at him but concentrate on Lily's face. He leaves quietly, closing the door.

"Are you here for her?" I ask, looking at the pretty little girl standing in the corner.

"Maybe," her voice tinkles sweetly.

"I won't let you take her."

That makes her smile but it's not a little girl smile. It's menacing.

"Maybe," her voice tinkles again.

I walk around to the side of the bed and lay down on my side, facing Lily, my back to the little girl.

"Are you staying?" I say, loud enough for the little girl to hear.

"Maybe."

I close my eyes and take a deep breath, pulling the air into my body. Lily's scent is here but barely. I follow the little bit left and remember what she told me last night, when everything was perfect, before Cindy was gone.

"Your words are of no value here. Show me how you feel."

I chase the sound of that voice and feel myself sliding away, caught in a warm afternoon wind. I find myself in a desert, flat except for some hills shimmering in the distance. Other than a few cacti, nothing grows among the rocks and dry earth. I start walking towards the hills and it's nearly dark before I reach them. I'm so thirsty and my skin feels raw. I start to climb, slipping several times on the loose rocks as the sky turns to black. By the time, I reach the top, the night has closed in all around me.

It's cold now and a mean wind swirls, scratching the rocks. I shout Lily's name over and over but the wind just carries it away each time. This isn't helping. I look around but my eyes can't focus on anything in the dark.

"I need light," I mutter, looking down at my feet.

The wind pauses for a second. I rub the back of my head and feel the grit in it, then bring my palm around my face to cover my mouth. My eyes widen. I let my hand fall away.

"Show me how you feel," I whisper.

I stand still as the wind picks up again.

"I don't need light. She does."

I grin broadly and imagine my white teeth glistening. I imagine that shine spreading across my face and then across my body until all of me is bright and shining. I think about a light bulb and the glow inside it. I think about summer and heat. I think about bees flying across a field, searching for nectar. I think about the yellow and white flowers in the little girl's hand.

And then I can see myself standing on the hilltop, glowing. I'm a light to guide Lily back. I can leave this place now and my energy will stay here, shining out in all directions. Maybe she'll feel my warmth and my feeling for her. I put everything I am into it and hope it's enough.

"These are for you," the little girl says sweetly.

I'm lying on my back and the little girl is standing beside the bed, looking down at me. She's holding out her red balloon and her flowers to me. I reach up, dazed, and take them from her.

"Thanks," I say, thickly. My throat is dry and my tongue feels like a lump in my mouth.

"You're welcome," she sings. "See you later, alligator."

I can't help myself from finishing the childish good-bye.

"In a while, crocodile," I murmur.

I blink and then sit up but she's already gone.

I look over at Lily. She's still the same.

I sigh and get up.

Bodie is waiting for me at the end of the hall. I hand him the balloon and the flowers before going into the kitchen. He follows me, studying the balloon and flowers closely but saying nothing. I rustle through the cupboards until I find a vase and fill it with water. He puts the flowers in the water and ties the string from the balloon around the handle of the vase.

"Bodie, can you go and sit with Lily, please? I have to go home for a little while. I have to tell my parents what happened to Cindy. Could you put the flowers by Lily?"

"Where did they come from?" he looks at me curiously.

"A friend, but I think you knew that already," I say flatly, heading past him to the front door. "I'll be back in a couple of hours."

I don't look back as I head out into the sunshine. The eyes of Cherry and Ruby are still close but they've changed. They're cautious now. They don't know what I'm up to. I don't either but I won't tell them that. I walk quickly towards my house, concentrating on what I have to do, trying to ignore their stare.

The smell of cooking is in the house when I walk through the door. The clock in the hallway says it's twenty minutes to six. I stand in the doorway, shocked. It took me hours to walk across the desert and it seems the same hours have gone by in the real world or whatever this place is. I imagine the light I've left on top of the hill. Is it still burning or is that just my hope? Death left me the balloon and flowers so I think I must have done something right. But she also said "see you later" so maybe she will see me later, when she comes to get Lily.

I shake my head quickly and shut the door. I have things to say and do here before I can go back to that place.

"Sam? Is that you?" Mom calls from the kitchen. "It's almost supper."

I become an actor in my own body. Dad's in the kitchen when I walk in so I tell them both about Cindy. Their reaction appears sincere so I must say the right things. Mom starts packing up some food for me to bring over to Bodie and Lily. I call Kathy's house. Pete gets on the other line and I talk to both of them for a minute. Kathy wants to see Lily but I say something about tomorrow and Kathy seems to think that's fine.

Sara walks in the room and Mom and Dad tell her what happened and she just stands there, stupid, looking blankly at me. Probably wondering if she's still going to get any attention out of all this. I'm too out of it to be annoyed at her for long.

I hang up the phone, hoping I said what I'm supposed to say. Mom is loading a cooler with sandwiches, juice boxes, cookies, God knows what else and Dad is telling her that there are just two of them and they don't need food for a week. Mom glares at him and he just shrugs his shoulders. Then he turns to me and asks me a question.

I don't answer.

"Sam," he says, walking up to me and scaring the crap out of me by giving me a hug. My father is holding me. Really, the world is coming to an end. "Are you staying there tonight?"

His hands are still on my arms and now he's looking into my face.

"Uh, yeah, sure."

"Good man," he says, patting me on the arm. He walks away. Even as out of it as I am, I'm caught off guard by his touchy-feely worrying.

Before I leave, Mom gives me some hugs and sloppy kisses on the cheek, tells me to send my love to Lily and says three times to call if they need anything. Dad has already loaded the cooler in the back of the van. On the drive over, he gives me some awkward advice about not talking too much, just being there will help. Since tomorrow is Friday, it's cool with him if I cut school. I just nod the whole way over.

Bodie meets us in the driveway. I carry the cooler inside while he makes conversation with Dad. I'm sure it's the same calm voice of reason Bodie gave Principal Atkinson. Everything is taken care of. Thank you for your concern. Lily is holding up well but she doesn't want to see anyone yet. She's a strong girl. She'll be ok. Yes, I will have Sam call if we need anything. There will be a memorial service next week.

I place the cooler on the kitchen counter before heading down the hallway to check on Lily. Beside her bed on her night table is the vase with the yellow and white flowers spilling out. The red balloon floats above the flowers like a sun.

Lily looks better. I can't see the bed through her body anymore but she still has this fuzziness when I look at her.

I head back to the kitchen and am halfway through unpacking the food from the cooler and putting the sandwiches and juice into the fridge when Bodie comes back in.

"Your father is proud of you," he says.

"Yeah, sure," I reply. I stack the sandwiches on the second shelf in the fridge so the juice can go on the top shelf.

"Lily is recovering."

"Yeah, it looks that way," I snap the lid to the empty cooler shut.

I start back down the hallway to Lily's room, two sandwiches in one hand and a juice box in the other.

He follows me into the bedroom. While I sit on the floor against the dresser on the opposite side of the room from Lily so I can have a clear view of her, Bodie walks over to examine the vase again. He sniffs the flowers and taps the balloon cautiously with a finger, making it sway in the air.

"You did not bring these here?"

"No, not really," I say through a big bite of ham sandwich with lettuce and pickle in it.

Now he turns to look at me.

"I am unaccustomed to bartering for information or to being uncertain about what is transpiring," he says, walking over and sitting down beside me. "You have some questions for me and I will answer them as best I can but I have some questions for you as well, Sam."

"Like what?" I slurp noisily from the juice box.

"Who brought the flowers and the balloon?" He isn't looking at me but Lily.

"I thought you would have figured it out. You were the one who said the death guardian was here. She's a nice little girl."

"She was in the room? She gave them to you? She spoke?"

"Yeah."

"I see."

"You see what?" I ask suspiciously, postponing another bite of sandwich.

"Please resume your meal, Sam, and I will speak for a few moments and then I must leave you for a short time. The guardian you call death has brought you and Lily a gift, an action unprecedented in the history of our kind. The steps you took this afternoon to restore Lily have helped her situation. I am…impressed."

He pauses. I take my last bite and lean my head back against the wall, staring out the window. It'll be dark in about an hour or so but the light is still pouring in strong.

"Amara wants you to be the end of everything. She was able to hide her intentions from Lily because she disguised her goal as revenge. She only thought of making Samael's dream real. She dreams of reuniting with Samael through you. She wants to die and she wants all things to die with her."

"Am I Samael?" I whisper. Saying his name feels strange, like just the word could cause trouble.

"No, you are yourself, Sam Gardner. You have been forged into a power Samael wishes he had possessed. You see the one we cannot and you have the ability to give her everything she desires. You are her harbinger."

He takes a breath to continue but I cut him off angrily.

"Forget it. I do have a lot of questions but I don't want you to answer them. I'm not sure I want the answers at all because the more I find out, the more mad I get. I've had it with my life being explained as some stupid game about somebody trying to get revenge by killing everything in the world. I just want Lily back for now and then I'll worry about the rest."

He nods but says nothing. We sit in silence for a minute and then he gets up.

"I will go now. I must appear before Amara. Cherry and Ruby see all but there are things they witness that they do not understand. Please do not be alarmed. I move freely among all the guardians and my duty is simply to share what I know. She will be…disappointed…with the information I possess. I shall return here after dawn. There are further arrangements in your world I must make."

Something snaps into place in my head, something Lily told me about how I was born like this.

"You were the one who told Amara what to do," I accuse him. "It was you who made me this way."

Bodie looks at me matter-of-factly, as if I just told him what town we were in.

"So? I share my knowledge with her and I share it with Lily and I share it with you now. I shared it with Cindy so she could make life itself. What are you asking me, Sam?"

"Ok," I say, looking at Lily on her bed and ignoring him. "Nothing."

He nods again and then leaves the room without saying anything.

I get to my feet and go lie beside Lily on the bed, facing her.

"Lily, you've got to come back," I whisper. "I don't

trust this Bodie guy. I think he's just hanging around because he's curious about how all this is going to end. I don't think he cares for you or for me."

She doesn't answer, of course. She just lies there on her back, looking peaceful but not quite there.

I don't touch her.

I sigh and stare at her.

The smell of the flowers fills the room.

Coffee (Amara)

The black liquid is hot and harsh in my mouth. Bodie has a smile on his face as he watches me process the sensation of taste. It is still new to me. I swallow and I smile back at him.

"It's beautiful."

"Of course it is," he nods.

I take another sip. The taste is complex. I lack the vocabulary to describe it and I have little to compare it with. When I took human form, I never thought about tasting anything because I don't feel the need to consume food. It's an unusual sense—taste—it communicates detailed information that defies proper explanation. I presume something foul tasting would tell me it is foul as much as this coffee tells me things about itself, hinting at the dark, dense secrets not available to anyone who does not taste it.

"How is it made?" I ask him.

"Coffee fruit is grown on trees and picked when ripe, the pit is then removed from the fruit and aged, ground into tiny pieces and then run through hot water," he answers.

I nod and sip again, glancing around this coffee shop,

this place where humans come to meet and consume coffee together. Living things, whether they are humans or trees that grow coffee, create interesting diversity but this is not how it should be. This is a blemish on the pure black stillness that makes up most of the universe. It cannot be allowed to continue.

Still, the coffee pleases me.

"Why are we here, Amara? Why have you come out of isolation? You despise these creatures." He tries to make his voice sound like he has no care for the answers but of course he does.

"You know why. You know I have been near this community and have been close to the human manifestation of Samael I have created. Your real question is why now. Our time is nearly over so I don't see any harm in indulging myself before the end."

I smile at Bodie. The sun shines through the window. A human male, about 19 years of age, looks at me from across the room and grins at me. I look at Bodie, uncertain how to behave.

"He thinks you are attractive," Bodie murmurs so the smiling human won't hear.

Now I smile back at the boy. I find our wordless encounter amusing. I am tempted to show him my light through my eyes. He would go immediately blind. His brain would finish evaporating a few seconds later.

"She has appeared to Sam," Bodie says urgently, trying to distract me from the boy.

I look back at Bodie, my smile remaining in place.

"That boy dies now or he dies later. What does it matter? He and his kind cannot outrun her."

"She presented Sam with a gift," he adds.

Bodie has confirmed what I only suspected could

happen. Death has appeared to Samael. This is wonderful news.

"Of course she did. She loves him. Rather than wait for the living to fall to her domain, he can bring them all to her."

"This was not your original plan," he says as his mouth opens to take more of his own coffee.

I lower my smile and look into the white cup. The beverage is gone and only the stain of what once occupied it lines the cup. I didn't know when death would appear, whether it would be at the beginning or at the end, but I knew she had to come. She will not have to wait long before he brings them to her. Before he brings everything to her.

Even me.

Especially me.

"Lilith will return?" I say into my cup.

"Later tonight or tomorrow, she will be one again. Sam rescued her."

Now I look at Bodie, holding out the cup.

"Can you get me another, please?"

He rises and dutifully walks to the counter. I consider him carefully. Even if Bodie tells Lilith that I wanted Samael to bring her back just so her love could be the one to betray her, she won't believe him. She came back to her Sam because she loves him. When he comes to me, she will make no effort to stop him.

I hope Bodie tells her what lies ahead. If she knows in advance that she is powerless to prevent what is to come, that will please me. Like this coffee Bodie presents to me, she will know the taste of my deception.

It is dark. It is burning. It is bitter.

Surfacing (Lily)

I want him.

I want to be near him forever.

I want him to heal me.

I want to nurture him.

I want.

I want.

I want.

I want.

My essence has never been this defined.

He wants me to come to him.

He wants to hold me to the rain to wash away all the hurt.

He wants to hold me to the sun to dry my tears.

He wants to kiss me on the mouth to bring me back to life.

He smells like a new life.

He tastes crisp and tart, a fresh apple from the tree.

Where I burn, he is a balm.

Where I ache, he is ointment.

I will earn his faith in me.

I will not disappoint him.

I will not forsake him to Amara and his fate.

All dressed up (Sam)

I carry the cooler and walk home. I need the warm fresh air and the sun on my face and the time to think about what happened.

Lily woke up this morning.

I can't think about that again or I'll start crying some more, right here in the middle of the street. I'm so relieved. She found my beacon and it helped bring her back. Whatever happens now we can face together. I'm still scared of what's ahead but at least I won't be alone.

She loved the flowers and the balloon. She took one of the white ones out of the vase and sniffed it constantly, sighing happily.

She was even happier when Bodie returned. They just looked at each other and smiled. Bodie stood at the end of the bed, unable to take his eyes off her as we sat there, holding hands. I wondered whether I had been too harsh on Bodie. His concern for Lily seemed genuine enough.

I didn't want to go but Bodie said it was time and Lily agreed, nodding her head. It seemed silly that we were going through the motions when Amara could make her move at any time but they both seemed satisfied that nothing was going to happen right away. Plus, Lily seemed very fragile. She was herself again but I could tell she was torn up inside. She nodded again, back to her confident self, her eyes shining at me.

So I kissed her and I left.

The eyes of Ruby and Cherry are further back but they follow me to my house and I realize they aren't interested in Lily but me. Amara is waiting to see what my next move will be. I won't play that game. The closer I get to the house, the calmer I feel. Lily is back and I feel comfortable in my skin again, like things can somehow return to normal.

I walk up the steps and put the cooler down. My arms are sore from walking that distance with something not that heavy but still awkward to carry. But I love the soreness. I love the sweat forming on my face. I need a shower. This is where I belong, in my little Sam world, with my hovering Mom and Dad, and my annoying sister, and my caring friends. I need to be thinking about school and exams and graduation and university.

I feel guilty but I even look forward to Cindy's funeral. Her death will be mourned by humans, in a human way. Bodie has arranged a cremation and a memorial for Wednesday, five days from now. I'm not sure what will be cremated, if it will actually be what remains of Cindy's human form, or if it will be just a body Bodie has somehow formed to take her place, but that doesn't matter. People who knew her will come together to remember her and that makes me feel better.

The door is locked so I grab the hidden key under the rock in the flower garden and let myself in. Mom and Dad are at work and Sara is at school. I grew up in this house and just to walk inside it feels like I'm putting on a comfortable pair of shoes. I call both of them at their offices and tell them I'm home. I can hear their love for me in their voices (and, of course, Mom says it out loud but Dad doesn't). They're happy I stayed with Lily and am so loyal and loving to her.

I tell them about the funeral arrangements Bodie has made so far. Mom asks me to bring Bodie and Lily over later for supper or just a coffee. "They shouldn't just sit in the house, that's not healthy," she frets. I agree with her because I know that will please her and say my goodbye.

I grab my mp3 player, turn on some heavy tunes to get my blood pumping and head out again. It's nearly lunch at school so I can grab Pete and Kathy. I drum on my legs as I walk quickly. I go past Lily's house but decide not to stop. After what I did to bring her back, I need a rest from her. I hope she doesn't see me walk by and feel hurt, wondering why I'm not coming in to check up on her. I don't have the energy to return to the danger and the uncertainty just yet.

Pete and Kathy see me from the street. I hear the bell ring and see students coming out of the doors and then, just as I approach the corner, they're running across the street to meet me. Kathy throws herself into my arms and I can't help but laugh. In her worried arms, I feel like she's squeezing out the part of me that's causing all this trouble, that has drawn me into this mess in the first place.

"What's so funny, man?" Pete asks with a puzzled look on his face. He isn't expecting laughs and smiles so soon.

Kathy steps back and looks at my face.

"It's great to see you guys," I say, slowly, looking at them both, emphasizing each word.

"Oh, Sam," Kathy is trying not to cry. She grabs Pete's arm for support. "How is Lily?"

"She's…"

I can't finish. All my happiness to be back in my Sam life has suddenly gone. Lily lost Cindy.

For the first time, I can feel what that must be like. I brought her back but that doesn't mean she's whole again. She's alone now in a way she has not been ever, for as long as she has been alive and I still can't really come to grips with how long that is. All I can remember was that snapping sound of Cindy's death and the cruelty and wrongness of it. Cindy's death was more than just losing a future together. For Lily, it's taking away someone that has been part of her. They were like Siamese twins and now one of them has died and has been hacked off like a piece of meat.

"She's…" I say, again, but it comes out wrong past my shaking lips. My chest feels so heavy.

Kathy is hugging me again and Pete comes and puts

his heavy arms around both of us.

"It's ok, man," he says, patting my shoulder. "I think we get it."

They get it then and they get it in the weeks to come.

They come by the house that day after school and the four of us go out for a walk down by the lake together. Lily is quiet but laughs a few times and smiles more than I thought she could. She holds my hand but keeps herself in her human form and I have no intention of making any move to draw her out until she's ready. Pete and Kathy are wonderful, of course. Even when they disagree, which isn't very often, they are playful. I feel so happy for both of them and I can feel Lily slowly coming around because of their gentle warmth.

Lily and Bodie come over to our house for supper on Sunday. In a completely different way, but just as thoroughly, Bodie charms the pants off my family, just like Cindy did at Christmas, though that feels so long ago now. I feel my nervousness towards Bodie starting to change to respect. He's a know-it-all, of course, but he also knows what he doesn't know, if that makes any sense. He's with Lily partly out of concern for her but it's also because of the uncertainty of me, of us, of the outcome of the situation. He loves the not knowing and he makes no effort to hide it.

"I know enough to know that nothing is certain and the past does not always dictate the future," he tells me one afternoon, a week or so after Cindy's funeral. "That is where hope resides."

At Cindy's memorial, the hall is packed. There's seating for 300 but there are people standing in the back and even outside. Students and teachers from school mix with dozens of parents with young children and more than a few expectant mothers. Lily sits in the front row next to me, expressionless. For the first time, I feel her presence reach out and it's terrible. She's aching for Cindy. She wants something back she can't have and that hurts. She still feels responsible. It's a flash, a whiff of her true self, a peek before she closes it off from me, squeezing my hand hard. She doesn't want me to help her carry her grief.

Bodie says some nice things during his short eulogy. He speaks to everyone but his eyes constantly come to back to Lily and me.

"Cindy's death made no sense in a world that makes no sense. Her life, however, made most sense because she devoted herself to beginnings. She helped women create new life, she encouraged men to want to create new life," he says, smiling and drawing a quiet laugh from everyone. No one there will ever forget Cindy's sensuality.

"She brought desire to life," he says, focusing on Lily and me. "She made our desperate yearning for love and for life and for happiness real, something tangible we could all hold close. She gave us the power to forge new beginnings of our own and that is her undying legacy."

Lily seems to take that message to heart, at least in her human world. She comes to school on the Monday after the funeral and throws herself into her books and especially her volunteer work. Except for walking her to school in the mornings, I don't see her much on weekdays. She's either doing homework or organizing the prom or bringing the yearbook together or fussing over gowns with Kathy.

On the weekends, we spend a lot of time with Pete and Kathy. As the spring turns into early summer, we go for picnics, see movies, badly play mini-golf, and even try an early season swim in the lake filled with the cold spring runoff from the mountains.

When we're alone, we're mostly quiet, lying on her bed in each other's arms. I hate that word cuddle because it seems so babyish but when Lily says 'let's go cuddle,' I can't think of anything that sounds better. Sometimes we just lie face to face and look at each other. She strokes my hair and I caress her cheek. More often, she likes to hold me in a protective embrace, like she did when she first came back after Cindy died, with my head on her chest. When I lift my head and look at her, I often see a fierce determination on her face, like she's concentrating on something far away.

"Are you okay? You look mad about something," I say the first time I see it.

She had been staring at the ceiling and now she looks at me. She takes my face in her hands and holds it tight, pressing her fingers around my jaw and against my ears.

"I love you so much, Sam, that there is nothing else I want but you," she says but her voice is cold and raw.

And then the room is gone and she's there, walking through a raging blizzard on an endless plain. She stumbles against the howling wind and the snow is falling sideways, blowing dry and cold into her face and her eyes. Each step is agony as her legs thrust knee deep into the snow. She trips and falls but she claws her way back to her feet and keeps moving. The wind blows so hard she has trouble catching her breath. Her lips are blue and her cheeks are drained of colour. She's so cold and so tired. Still, she keeps coming and I know she will never stop coming to me, even if that storm blows for the rest of time.

Her icy hands squeeze my face and her thumbs press lightly against my closed eyes.

"Do you see, Sam?"

She takes her thumbs off my eyes.

"Yeah," I say, my free hand coming on top of one of her hands on my face. She's so cold.

"I will never abandon you," she says, pausing at the word 'never', squeezing her hands on my face even more for emphasis.

Then she smiles and the coldness falls from her skin but I can still feel it on my face.

That's when an idea comes to me.

Even while studying for final exams and trying on a tuxedo to rent for the prom, I think about my plan. I haven't written anything since that Christmas night when Cindy and Lily tried to kill me and I found out what I was, or what I wasn't, but now I'm writing again. I start sketching out a plan to end all of this, to reach out to Cherry and Ruby, to speak to Amara and make a deal so Lily and I can be free.

I can't tell Lily because I know she'll never approve but I feel I have to try and the more I think about it, the more I know it's what I have to do.

Bodie is right about new beginnings. I'll make one for me and Lily.

I'll go see Amara.

I'll offer her the power she has given me back to her, so I can be human again.

And if she doesn't accept my gift, my peace offering, if she won't promise to leave Lily alone, I'll kill Amara myself.

Coffee (Lily)

"Wonderful," I smile and close my eyes, savouring

the taste.

"Amara sat in that very seat recently and said she enjoyed the coffee, too," Bodie says with a glint in his eye. He is happy to be telling me something that will startle me.

I try to hold the shock in but I cannot. I put down my cup and look around the room. At the far end, there is the hiss of milk being steamed. Many of the tables have people sitting in them, chatting with others, reading alone, tapping their laptops. They seem calm and relaxed.

I wish I was them.

Amara was here in human form? She is stalking me.

No.

Not me. Him.

She feels him.

Sam wants her.

He wants to find Amara.

He wants Amara to leave me alone.

I have felt it. His wants are plain to me, whether he'll admit them even to himself.

"You need to decide," Bodie disrupts my thoughts with his cool logic.

"My decision is to make no decision. Sam will decide," I say through my gritted teeth, staring at him.

"You will put his wants over your own? You could die. We could all die." Bodie sounds surprised. His face betrays it.

"You could still kill him. You know how," he adds, hopefully.

There is nothing to say to that. It is too late for words.

Sam will make his choice.

If he chooses what Amara means for him to be, I will be ready.

Stoke (Amara)

On the steps, I brief Kyle and Dan again about their assignment. They leave with even more anticipation than when I set them loose on Cindy.

I return to my room and close the door, shutting out the sun and the wind and the water and the sand.

The room is dark, except for the hot coals in the hearth. I throw on more wood and rebuild the fire until it is crackling with pleasure.

I sit in my chair and sigh.

Finally, he is coming.

The closer he gets, the deeper the ache of my loneliness becomes.

I do not care anymore that Lily feels me wanting him because she is unable to prevent his evolution.

There is only one thing left separating him from what he is.

It will burn in this fire.

Gifts (Sam)

Graduation arrives but I'm distracted. Mom fusses over me, Dad shoots some video and Sara sulks, arms crossed under a frown. I win a scholarship to the University of Northern British Columbia in Prince George to study environmental engineering. I don't remember even applying. Mom is already arranging for me to stay in the basement suite of some friend of hers while I study there. It's hard to concentrate on September when I'm not sure if I'll survive June.

Still, I find a way to have a great time and the formal with Lily is nice. She looks perfect in her purple gown. I have to laugh when Mom says she looks so grown up.

Mom glares at me and I turn away. How can I not laugh when someone older than the universe gets told they look grown up? What am I supposed to do?

Even Bodie puts on a suit, a light grey spring suit that Lily picked out for him. He shaves and combs his hair, tying it in a neat ponytail. He looks like a corporate hippie. He confesses to me that he's enjoying being around humans more and more but he's also talking about moving on soon, whatever that means.

I finalize my plans at the same time as I write my last exams. Strangely, it seems to help me focus better on studying and all the time spent huddled over textbooks means I have an excuse to ignore Lily a little bit. She senses something is off about me but so far she has just chalked it up to the end of high school and the stress of waiting for Amara's next move.

Lily has tried to talk to me about it a couple of times but I've brushed her off. I know if we get talking, I won't be able to keep my secret from her. I can't bring Cindy back for her but I can try and bring her some safety. As the Thursday of my last exam approaches, I start avoiding Bodie more because it seems he suspects even more than Lily that I'm up to something. He keeps trying to draw me into these deep philosophical conversations about life and death and knowledge and uncertainty. He's hoping I'll accidentally tell him where my real thoughts are.

I write the geography exam in the morning and know I did well on it but I've forgotten everything by the time I walk out the school's front door. I know Lily is with Kathy in the library, preparing for their English final in the afternoon. I asked Lily if she's getting tired of being high school age in her human form and having to go through school and exams over and over and over. She looked at me like I was crazy.

"This is what I am, Sam," she said, more seriously than I expected. "Guardians don't get to choose their human forms. We just seem to settle in them. I think it has something to do with how people see us. You'd have to ask Bodie more about that."

She paused and bit her lip.

"The repetition of being human can be tiring. I took it for granted for too long but never again. Finding you and losing Cindy are my reminders that the effort to act human is not just a game or pretending to be something I'm not. Trying to be human is what makes me human. Discovering new depths of my humanity is endless and that pleases me."

I think about what she said as I walk as fast as I can home. I realize I have selfish reasons for wanting to work out a deal with Amara. I don't want this power because I still feel I could hurt Lily and everyone if something went wrong. I don't want that responsibility. I want to be myself again. I don't know if what I have inside me makes me immortal like Lily. Even Bodie isn't sure so the idea that I could get old and die while Lily would be a teenager forever makes me sad but I can live with it. Being human comes with a cost and I know no one knows that as well as Lily does. She'll be angry with me if my plan works but I know she'll understand what I was trying to do.

Bodie and his convertible are waiting for me in front of the house. He's leaning against the driver's door.

"Hey, what's up?" I say, walking up to him, trying to be as casual as possible.

"I will take you to her now," he says, his face stern and serious.

"What? Who?" I say, playing dumb.

"Sam, do not insult me," he says, standing right in front of my face. "I know you mean to end this current stalemate between Lily and Amara."

He pauses and I do my best poker face, staring right back at him.

"It was not wise of you to make notes," he says quietly, holding up a handful of papers. "But even if you hadn't, I would still have known."

I look away, shaking my head. I can stand here all afternoon arguing with Bodie that they are just random thoughts and don't mean anything or I'm waiting to talk to Lily about it or some other half-baked story. I could freak out about how he looked through my things, invading my privacy but I know it'll all be a waste of time. He knows the truth. There'll be no other opportunity like this, with Lily out of the way and focused on the human world, for me to reach out to Amara.

"She knows, you know. How could Lily not know? You want this to happen." Bodie interrupts my thoughts.

I look behind me, scared that she might be coming but the street is empty. I stare at Bodie, angry that he knows everything.

"She will not interfere because she wants you to find your way. I disagree but she has decided." His voice is flat and frustrated.

I look past Bodie to the mountain tops to the west and south of Kelowna. Some large clouds have cast a deep shadow over them, even though it's still a mostly sunny and warm day. The fact that Lily knows but said nothing to talk me out of it gives me the last push of confidence I need.

"Drive me there, then," I say, trying to sound sure.

He snorts in disgust and shakes his head. Then he

turns to the car, opening his door.

"Get in," he spits out as he takes the driver's seat. I can't be sure but I think he's muttering under his breath as I walk around to the other side of the car and climb inside. The words moron and idiot seem to be in the air.

We don't talk at all on the drive. He heads south on Richter Street to Lakeshore Road at his usual slow and careful pace so I have time to savour the view of the lake and West Kelowna and Peachland across the water. Everything is all green and lush. Boats are cutting arcs across the water. A jet ski throws spray into the air, making small rainbows.

The car kicks up a cloud of dust as we finally leave the pavement, still heading south. The undergrowth is green but the trees still standing are black, charred by a forest fire from when I was a kid. There are only a few homes here but they are new and huge and secluded, down below the road and close to the water. Bodie comes to a quick stop at the top of a driveway on the right and leaves the motor running. The dust catches up to us and sweeps over the car but he doesn't seem to care.

"Are you getting out?" he asks when I don't move.

I don't want to look at him and give him the satisfaction of my fear and indecision so I stumble out and slam the door to show him I'm not scared or unsure.

"If we do not meet again, Sam Gardner, the pleasure has been mine," he says, barely loud enough over the crunch of the tires on the dirt and rocks as he backs up and turns the car north towards the city.

"Hey, where are you going?" I shout. "How am I supposed to get home?"

He doesn't look back as he throws the car into drive. Again, I just barely hear him as the car moves away.

"I will bring Lily here after her examination at school has concluded. She will need to be with you, one way or the other," his voice carries to me. In seconds, the car is around the corner and the quiet of the nearby water and what's left of the forest takes over.

I start walking down the steep driveway towards the water. The air is still except for little gusts of a breeze. I don't look at the few trees on either side but concentrate on the path in front of me. I'm being watched. It feels like I'm walking down a deserted back alley at night.

I have a sweat forming on my face as the driveway gently curls northward, hugging the hillside and avoiding the narrow ravine cut into its side.

"Hey, boyfriend, you made it."

"Just in time, too."

Cherry and Ruby are standing just ahead. Their giggle puts me on edge. I want them to shut up.

I stop and glare at them.

"You're here for Amara, aren't you?"

"But let's get a good look at you first."

And then they're gone.

Now they are two pairs of eyes looming over me, huge and unblinking, cutting right through me. I fall, hitting my head hard on the gravel, cutting my face, but the pain doesn't register. Cherry and Ruby's focus on me won't stop. They are cutting me open like a frog in a high school biology experiment. I'm spilling my guts to them in flashes. Not just my life but every passing thought, every idea, every dream, every fantasy I've ever had comes to the surface in one huge wave.

I'm drowning, ashamed with what I see.

My jealousy of Pete is there and I see myself taking Kathy for myself and she worships me. She's on top of me, pulling her shirt off, kissing me, telling me how I'm so much more than little sad Pete.

Mom and Dad only see my victories, my accomplishments. They tell Sara what a ridiculous, pathetic thing she is and how we all would have better off if she hadn't been born. Her misery makes us all laugh.

There are all the petty injustices and outrages of my childhood. Kids who made fun of me are humiliated and rejected. Teachers who scolded me are found standing in front of the class with no clothes on. They whimper as we beat them with our wooden rulers.

I'm filled with disgust at myself. In my shame, I try to make myself smaller but Cherry and Ruby only open me up wider.

Now I'm torturing Lily. We're in the special place we found together the night Cindy died. I'm on a beach and I hold a crystal with her inside of it. I break pieces of it off and throw them into the water and she's screaming, begging for me to stop, promising me anything I want if I would only have mercy.

The only thing I want is for her to keep crying out in agony forever because it sounds like the sweetest music I've ever heard.

This last sight is too much. From a faraway place, I hear an angry yell and realize it's me. I feel my hands claw into the air, each finger a knife and I close them tight.

I'm still lying on the driveway, dangerously close to the rocky edge that falls off steeply below me into the ravine leading down to the lake. My arms won't stop shaking and my hands are balled into tight, bloody fists.

"Can I have those, please?" the little girl asks sweetly.

I turn, startled and jump to my feet. My arms can't stop jerking as whatever is in my hands is fighting to get out. The little girl is wearing the same Sunday-best outfit as before, when I saw her at Lily's house. She looks at me expectantly as she pops a bright red lollipop back into her mouth. It clatters against her teeth and her tongue makes smacking noises around it.

I bring my shaking fists up so I can look at them. They're drenched in blood but I know it's not mine. I squeeze even tighter. Blood oozes out of the sides and finally whatever is inside my hands stops moving.

"Are you done with those because I'd like to have them," the little girl says.

I open my hands to see what she wants.

Resting in each palm are two sopping eyeballs. They turn jerkily this way and that before focusing on my face. They look up at me in absolute terror.

"Cherry," I whisper, looking at one set of eyes and then the other. "Ruby."

Past their fear of me and the little girl, I can see what they had seen in me and I clench my teeth, sucking in the air through my nose in anger. They've seen every last pathetic human side of me and rubbed my face in the stink of every one of those moments and thoughts. No one can know those things about me, those things I worked so hard to push deep down and hide.

I hold out my hands to the little girl.

She smiles at me and steps forward.

I place the eyes into her perfect pink hands without hesitation.

Her small fingers close around them.

"Thank you," she says through her lollipop, looking up at me, her face beaming. "You're so nice."

I want nothing more than to bring more gifts to that little girl, to keep giving and giving to her until there's nothing left anywhere to give and then I would give myself to her. A sweet little angel like this deserves a big brother who'll look out for her and give her everything she deserves. I can see all the presents I could give her, wrapped perfectly in bright paper, stuffed underneath a giant, shiny tree. There would be so many presents and some would be so big they couldn't fit under the tree so they'll sit to the side, shimmering in the blinking lights.

She'll open all the gifts and everything will be wonderful.

"Can I stay with you?" she asks.

I open my mouth but I can't talk. I'm breathing in short gasps and my chest aches. I put my hand over it, trying to make it stop hurting, trying to catch my breath.

"You don't want me to come with you?" she asks, her face now twisted into a deep adorable sadness. Her lip is pulled up in a cute little pout.

"You can't," I gasp. My chest is tightening in spasms. "No, no, you can't."

She turns her mouth sideways, in a little grimace of regret.

Then her face brightens again.

"That's ok. Maybe some other time."

She turns and skips up the driveway away from me.

"See you later, alligator," she calls over her shoulder.

"In a while, crocodile," I choke, falling to my knees.

I hunch forward at the waist, my arms pulled tightly to my chest but the pain just intensifies.

I open my eyes. They're looking down at the ground but instead of dirt, I see two pairs of feet. The ones to the left are elegant black dress shoes, laced and knotted perfectly. The other two feet are covered with scuffed camouflage dark green military-style boots.

A hand closes over my hair and pulls me up straight. I shout in shock at the new pain.

The last thing I hear is the wet clap of a heavy fist hammering my face.

In human (Lily)

Bodie has just run a red light, swerving to avoid a collision.

"Asshole," he curses, throwing a finger in the air.

He is not as skilled at driving fast as Cindy but he feels the need to do so now as he drives us south along the lake.

I do not move in the seat as the tires complain shrilly. Bodie steers around a sharp corner, hitting the gas pedal hard. There is no need to rush but I say nothing to Bodie.

Sam needs me now. I must save him.

He will make his choice and I must be there to save him from whatever he decides.

In Sam lie all the answers.

I remember when I returned to my human form after Cindy died and he was there.

He was stroking my face.

"Welcome back," he whispered.

He was crying.

I was flooded with his joy and I was crying, too.

He laid his head on my chest.

There was no heart underneath my breast but he heard one beating nevertheless.

"Hello," I said, holding his head down against me.

"I am home."

Now it's my turn to guide him home.

Inhuman (Sam)

"My name is Kyle," says a nicely dressed man of about 30 years old in a spotless dark suit. He's laying my head into an iron vice. "I am the guardian who controls power."

"My name is Dan," says the other man, about the same age, dressed in khaki pants and a desert camouflage T-shirt that can't fully contain his muscular chest and arms. "I am the guardian in charge of strength."

He's methodically beating my legs with a solid steel pipe.

I'm screaming but I can't hear myself as the vice is pressed tightly against my ears. I can't concentrate or relax long enough to let myself go, to escape this place, to find Lily. Whenever I think I might be slipping away, Dan crunches the metal pipe into my genitals or Kyle gives the vice another half turn, squeezing my head harder. I can't breathe. My skull is making crunching sounds.

This goes on for hours. I lose track. There are flashing lights in my face, so bright they hurt even when my eyes are closed. They tilt me backwards, place a wet cloth over my face and pour ice cold water over me. I'm puking and drowning at the same time in my own vomit. I smell something burning and realize they're laying a red-hot poker on my stomach. My body starts shaking uncontrollably and my eyes roll to the back of my head when they hook up electrodes to my testicles and connect them to a car battery. I watch Dan pull out every one of my fingernails and toenails with needle-nosed pliers.

Every part of me is shivering and sweating and oozing blood and pain but what Kyle and Dan are doing to me is a distraction. They aren't touching the pain inside my chest yet. My ribs feel like they're being slowly broken as something is pushing out of me, something desperate to get out. Every breath reminds me my lungs are filled with fire.

"This is what it felt like," Kyle informs me as he uses a pair of pruning sheers to clip my nostrils and the top, bottom and sides of my mouth.

"For Cherry and Ruby in your hands," Dan finishes as he brings down a sledgehammer onto my ankles and feet. The bones inside sound like a stack of ceramic plates shattering on a concrete floor.

The pain in my chest flares even more.

I killed Cherry and Ruby. I killed two guardians.

I did it not because they were trying to kill me or hurt Lily. I did it out of guilt, out of shame. I did it because I could. I murdered them and it felt so easy and so right. What's happening to me? Lily warned me but I didn't listen. Bodie told me what Amara had planned for me but I thought I was in control. Something in me shouts through the pain.

If I could escape being tied to this operating table, I would do it to Kyle and Dan, just like I had to Cherry and Ruby. I know I can. I have the power and the strength.

"Really?" Kyle says, loosening the vice so I can move my head.

"Why don't you try?" Dan says, unshackling the metal cuffs off my hands and feet.

"You can do it," Kyle says, stepping back.

"Come on. Get up. Give us your best," Dan says, standing beside Kyle.

I try pushing myself up and fall off the table instead. I can't bring my hands up fast enough to cushion my fall so my face slams into the floor. Blood sprays out as my nose breaks.

"Good effort," Kyle says, above me.

"Not bad," Dan acknowledges.

Lying face down, I can see the little girl in the corner of the room. She's juggling four white balls, her tongue poking out of the side of her mouth in concentration. The balls flow between her hands and fly through the air but she's having trouble. Finally, one falls and hits the floor, breaking like an egg, oozing its red gooey insides out. Then another falls and finally the other two.

She stares at the mess on the floor, sadly.

Then she brings her face up, meets my stare and smiles.

"I broke my toys but I know you have more for me," she says.

"I can't," I croak through my battered mouth.

"Don't be a silly willy," she grins. "You can do whatever you want."

"They're…hurting me," I say, coughing out blood.

She brings her hand to her mouth and giggles through it.

"These guys? They're just playing. They can't hurt you."

I reach out a hand to her. It shakes in the air from the effort.

"Take me," I beg.

She stops laughing and looks at me seriously.

"Now I told you to stop being a silly willy," she says, scolding me, her little forefinger wagging at me like a whip. "Don't be a baby about everything."

"Please," I'm starting to crawl towards her.

The little girl's face darkens. She crosses her arms and looks away from me.

"You were so nice before and now you're so mean. I thought you were my friend. I want you to bring me more toys," her voice is shrill and she stomps her little black shoe for emphasis.

I groan and pull myself to my hands and knees.

"I think he is ready now," Kyle says, standing on one side of me.

"I believe you are correct," Dan adds, standing on the other side.

They each grab an arm and yank me to my feet, holding me up.

The little girl glares at me sulkily.

"I hope I never see you again," she whines.

"Yeah, sure." I don't believe her.

The two men drag me through a doorway and into a warm, dark room. They sit me up on an old, well-used brown couch and leave. The only light is coming from a fireplace on the other side of the room, which contains a large, crackling fire. In front of the fire is the shape of a girl, my age, sitting relaxed, slowly moving in a wooden rocking chair. I can only see her silhouette and the light of the fire shines around her like a halo.

"Hello," she says in a soft delicate voice that reminds me of oatmeal cookies sitting on a cooling pan, fresh out of the oven. "My name is Amara and I have been looking forward to meeting you."

My eyes widen but I say nothing. I'm not sure what I expected of Amara, who I had been told was this horrible creature out to destroy the universe, and everyone in it, starting with Lily. Yet this girl sitting on a rocking chair, which makes soft creaking noises as it smoothly moves back and forth on a thick oval rug, is kind and warm. I want her to give me a hot bowl of chicken soup with pasta and vegetables in it. I'd bend my head down to the bowl and shovel the soup into my mouth, burning my tongue, but it would be so good.

I'm so tired and so hungry. It would be exactly what I

need.

"You have so much potential," she says, staring into the fire. "What are you waiting for? I am counting on you."

"What do you want?" I murmur, confused. I can't see this gentle girl killing Cindy or anyone or anything.

She finally turns to look at me. Her eyes are warm with kindness.

"I just want you to be you."

I try to sit up but I can barely move. My body is broken and the aching in my chest is now a roaring engine, a fist pounding at me from the inside out.

"Let me help you," she says, standing up. For one hopeful moment, I mistake her for Lily but she's a little taller, a little thinner. She's wearing jeans and a white T-shirt. Her hair, so blonde it looks nearly white, falls halfway down her back. She's natural and elegant.

She walks over and looks down at me. I try to smile but the cuts Kyle has made into my mouth and nose twist my face. By trying to move, I just slide down the couch, slumping.

"Stay right there," she tells me.

She puts her right knee down beside me and then, lifting herself over me, places her left knee on the other side so she's straddling me. She squeezes her thighs into my hips and lets her weight down onto me. I can't help myself from getting excited.

She just smiles. Her hair comes down in thick glowing waves past her shoulders. It makes her look like Cindy, except much younger and brighter.

I try to protest but she leans forward and pushes a sweet, affectionate finger against my torn lips.

"Shush. This won't hurt at all."

She starts undoing the buttons of my shirt, her fingers

working efficiently even though the buttons are slippery with blood. She looks at me with soft eyes the whole time and I can't look away. She opens my shirt to reveal my chest. Unlike the rest of me, it's whole, not cut or broken. It's the only part of me Kyle and Dan didn't touch.

"Ooh," she purrs, looking at her hands as her fingers graze delicately across my skin.

I try to move again but the best I can do is put my hands on her hips. She has me pinned securely. I can't get up or roll over.

"Samael," she whispers passionately. "I have waited so long for this."

Both of her hands break through the skin. She tears my ribs aside as if they're tissue paper hiding a gift below. I should be screaming or dying or something but instead I feel a burst of energy. All my pain is gone away. There's no blood. All the wounds Kyle and Dan gave me are gone and, best of all, the hurting inside my chest left as soon as she put her hands in me. I sigh with relief as the pressure that had been inside leaves me.

Amara's eyes are closed and her head is back. She's gasping with pleasure. Her hands are deep in my chest and I feel her for the first time, inside of me, a soft light, spreading everywhere. I'm standing on a grassy plain at dawn, looking to the east as the sun starts cresting the horizon. The sky is a perfect deep blue that leads down into rosy pink and finally a rich red, bursting with colour and promise.

And then the first hint of the sun creeps up, the top of the crescent reaching my eyes, and I can't stop staring into it, rejoicing at such beauty. This is the moment I have waited for all my life. I can see everything for the first time.

"Hold that thought," she says, leaning down to whisper in my ear. "You have a little something that's getting in our way."

As she stands up, I feel a sharp tugging as her hands come out of the darkness of my chest. There's a pulling sensation, followed by a ripping sound.

"There we go," she says, looking down at the pale, withered lump in her hands. It's dry and shrivelled, bloodless and cold.

As she walks across the room to the fire, there are several violent thumps in the room next door. They are loud and harsh. Then, a door opens.

The little girl runs into the room, ecstatic.

"Look, look, look," she cheers, racing up to me. Her arms are carrying Kyle's shoes and Dan's boots.

"Isn't this wonderful? I found some shoes and some boots to play with."

The little girl drops them on the ground in front of me. She kicks off her little shoes and places them on the couch beside me. She slips her feet into Kyle's shoes and her hands into Dan's boots and starts walking around on the room on all fours.

"I'm a horse, running on the prairie, see me run," she says joyfully, the boots and shoes slapping and scraping against the wooden floor.

"Amara, you will give what you have in your hands back to me if you value your existence."

The voice sounds like it might be Lily's and the figure standing in the doorway looks like it might be Lily but I can't be sure. She stands there, leaning forward, shoulders hunched around torn and bloodied clothes, her hands clenched in fists at her side. Into the room with her comes a horrible smell of something old and moldy and rotten. She's a carton of milk that has been left open on the counter for months, all green and black inside, gross with decay. I'm disgusted at the sight of her.

Amara turns to Lily and smiles.

"This old thing? Who wants that?"

She turns back to the fire and, with one motion, throws it into the blaze.

"No, no," Lily is running, not to Amara but towards me. Her eyes are filled with panic.

The instant what is left of my heart hits the fire, the room explodes with white light.

I jump to my feet and shout in triumph, soaking up every beam. I'm washed, I'm clean, I'm reborn and baptized. Everything weak and wrong inside of me has been cleaned away. I feel so strong and whole that the light seems to be streaming out of my fingers and toes. I'm glowing.

"Samael, you are magnificent," says Amara, walking to me with adoring eyes.

I smile and hold out a hand to her.

She takes it and I squeeze, pulling her close to me.

"Thank you for releasing me," I breathe, staring into her eyes.

"Anything for you, my Samael," Amara weeps. "Anything, my love."

I hear a moan to my side and turn in that direction.

Lily is lying, filthy and pathetic, face down on the floor. She looks up at me. There are tears in her eyes, too, but they're ugly. They cut angry red marks down her dirty cheeks.

"Sam," she cries, "Sam, no. This isn't you."

I look back at Amara, squeeze her hand and smile again at her.

"No," I say, looking down again at Lily, narrowing my eyes to focus on her sad figure sprawling on the floor. "This isn't Sam at all. This is better."

I close my eyes and take a deep breath, pulling in that repulsive stench and everything else of Lily's essence with it.

I hear the little girl laughing with glee.

I hear a young woman screaming.

It all sounds like sweet music.

Dawn (Amara)

I hold his hand and I am new again.

I feel his strength and know he will take me in and never let me go.

I am prepared for the eradication.

Time will finally end and everything will be quiet and perfect.

Mourning at the beach (Lily)

I betrayed Sam when I tore out his heart.

I gave it back to him and begged for his forgiveness.

Now he has betrayed me and himself.

I want him to come back to me, to come back to life.

I want him to want to live again.

Morning at the beach (Sam)

When I was 11 years old, we went on a family vacation to Mexico. We stayed at this place by the ocean but we were told to only go swimming in the pools at the resort. The ocean had dangerous undertows, we were warned, so we had to stay away.

The attraction of beaches for me was never the water anyway. I was the kid who preferred to stay on land, building sandcastles, complete with their own moat and a drawbridge made out of popsicle sticks or whatever debris I could find lying around. If I wasn't working on a sandcastle, I was scouring the sand for shells or money. If Dad would let me, I'd bury him in sand until just his head was sticking out.

So here I am on a beach by the water again, except this isn't the west coast of Mexico, it's the cool, dark waters of Okanagan Lake in front of me. It's late afternoon and there's a light breeze carrying the clean wet scent into me. The beach ends a short distance to my left in a sharp rise of sandy rock. A further distance away on my right, the trees have crept right down to the water. We are in a tiny cove. Behind me, the cabin sits empty and, beyond that, the driveway begins its steep climb towards the road where Bodie dropped me off.

I'm wearing the clothes I was when I came here but there's no sign on them or my body of what Kyle and Dan put me through. My thin plaid grey shirt is clean and bare. My jeans are not torn. I sit there on the sand, about 30 feet from where the waves reach the shore. I'm humming a nonsense song that has no rhythm to it, not really paying attention.

Behind me, her delicate but steady hands caressing my shoulders and neck, Amara bathes me in warmth.

"I was wrong," says the little girl, sitting down on my side, staring at me. "I really like you."

I look down at her and smile. The sun is burning bright overhead. It's a day filled with new beginnings and new possibilities. The opportunities are endless.

"Can I stay with you now?" she asks with a touch of pleading in her voice.

"You can always stay with me," I say, putting an arm around her, reassuring her.

"That's nice," she smiles back but I don't really see her mouth or her eyes. Lying past her, a short distance away, something lands in the sand, thrown from behind us. It rolls once and stops abruptly.

I get up and go to it, fascinated. It looks like a rock but it doesn't weigh much when I pick it up. It seems a lump of dried-out wood.

"Does it look familiar?"

At first, I think the voice is Amara and I turn to answer her. It's Lily, standing behind the little girl and Amara. Both of them are now on their feet. The little girl stares at Lily with a scowl while Amara has a curious expression on her face, as if she admires Lily.

"But I…" I stare at her and the realization sinks in of what I had done in the cabin, before we came outside. I tried to kill her. I did kill her.

I thought I had.

"How…?"

"Amara cast your heart into the blaze but there is no flame that could consume all of it," she says, walking up to me, ignoring the other two.

I stare down and see the thing I picked up in the sand is my heart but dried out and dead. I look at Amara.

"I thought you burned this," I say to her, confused.

"I did, or so I believed," she answers, looking at Lily instead of me. "You put a small piece of yourself in it, when you held it in your hands, before you gave it back to him."

"Just in case," Lily replies.

She turns to me.

"You have forsaken your humanity, Sam, and embraced what Amara means for you to become," Lily tilts her head towards Amara but doesn't acknowledge her. "She waits for you to give her and me to the guardian of death. I cannot see death but I know she is here with us."

"She's talking about me," the little girl says brightly.

"I can see her, you know," I say to Lily. "I met the little girl after Cindy died, while waiting for you to come back."

Lily nods slowly but says nothing.

"She is standing beside you," I looks at the little girl, who smiles sweetly back at me. "She's a cute little girl who loves it when I give her gifts to play with. She wants you."

"But not that lumpy bumpy thing you got," the little girl adds quickly, staring at what's in my hands.

"No, not this lumpy bumpy thing," I add, nodding. "It's junk."

"She speaks to you as well?" Lily asks.

The little girl turns to Lily and sticks her tongue out, making me laugh.

"She talks to me, she sticks her tongue out at you," I say, chuckling.

Lily stares at me but does not smile.

"So what do you want? Why are you here?" I say, annoyed that Lily hasn't found the situation at least a little funny.

Lily steps closer to Amara, who watches her carefully. "Like Amara, I want you to decide, Sam. It is time for you to choose between the love I still believe you have for me and the destiny she has made for you."

"Do I have to fight you?" I ask, worried. Even now

there's something about Lily wild and untamed that I feel is beyond my reach.

She smiles.

"I told you before, Sam. I would see you destroy the entire universe and all of the life within it before I could lift a hand against you."

I smile back at her and walk over to the little girl.

"If you want to give me up to my death, you need to hand me to her directly," Lily says, coming up beside me and taking my empty hand.

I look into Lily's face and hesitate. It's like she wants this. She wants me to give her away. Then I look down and see the little girl and her pretty face, beaming up at me. She adores me.

I look back at Lily.

I see in her face everything I wanted, everything I loved, but it seems far away now.

"You grabbed my hand like this just before you and Cindy tried to kill me," I say to her, my voice splintering. "How can I ever believe in you again?"

She squeezes my hand harder.

"I spared your life even after I knew what you were, even after Cindy," she replies, fighting to keep her words steady. "I fought for you. I never stopped believing in you. I want you."

I lower my head, shaking it slowly.

"I don't believe you."

I pull forward Lily's hand so the little girl can reach it.

She reaches for Lily's hand greedily.

The sun is suddenly covered in thick clouds where there had been none before. The wind blows harsh and cold, kicking up the sand around us. The lake churns mean and menacing. Lily has stepped between the little girl and me.

She has taken the little girl's hand and is holding on tight. The little girl is yelling at Lily to let go. She begins kicking Lily in the shin.

"You let go, you let go, I want you to stop, you can't do this, you let go right now," she whines, her voice rising in anger.

"I want you to let go. I said LET GO OF ME!" The little girl is screaming and crying now.

Lily looks into my face calmly. "I said I would never fight you, Sam, but I also said I would never abandon you," she turns from me back towards the little girl.

"Not to this," Lily murmurs coldly. She lets go of the little girl's hand. The little girl stumbles back, caught off guard. Then Lily raises her hand and backhands the little girl across the face so hard, it knocks her off her feet.

"I see you now, little one, and I am not afraid," Lily says, coolly studying the little girl sitting in shock on the sand.

The little girl looks up, her cheek red from the slap, tears in her eyes. Her face twists, her skin turns red and her lips begin to tremble. Finally, she takes in a long breath and begins wailing, covering her face.

Lily turns to me, tilting her head. She has a little smirk on her face as she sees how confused I am with what just happened.

"I have no time at the moment to explain how stupid you are, Sam," she says, laying extra emphasis on the word stupid. "You have not made it easy for me to save me from yourself." She squeezes my hand once more, then lets go of it, her face turning serious.

She steps around me. I turn to see Amara standing there, shaking. She looks so sweet and so sad. Lily stands between us.

"I am ready for you, Amara," Lily says with a cool threat in her voice. "Let us settle this or are you afraid of facing me alone?"

Amara just stands there. She is close to tears, looking first at Lily, then at me, then back at Lily.

"I don't want to fight you, sister Lilith. I never have. You should know that most of all. We have both lost so much. You know what it is that I really want," she says, looking at me again.

There is such deep longing in her eyes for me that my feet want to run to her. She needs me so much.

"You can't have him, Amara," Lily replies quietly. "He's mine."

Her voice stakes its claim on me with such intensity that I look away from Amara to her. She is still staring at Amara.

"My Samael," Amara pleads to me.

"Not yours," I reply. "And not yours, either, Lily."

I turn away from both of them, walk to the little girl and kneel on one knee in front of her. She has stopped crying but she's whimpering and rubbing her eyes with her fists.

"I'm sorry I have nothing else to give you right now, except for this," I say, holding out what remains of my shrunken and wasted heart, a trophy to make her smile again.

The little girl looks at me, shaking her head.

"I can't take that," she whispers.

"It's not mine anymore. I don't deserve it," I say, not looking down at it. "It belongs to you now."

Pouting, she shakes her head several times very quickly.

I look down at the heart. Taking it in both hands, I raise it to my mouth and blow on it gently. A redness surges through it and it begins to beat again slowly.

"Now," I say, holding it out to the little girl again. "It's fixed. See, it's not broken anymore."

The little girl stands up and takes my heart away with slow gentle hands. She kisses me lightly on the forehead, her lips smooth and dry.

"This is the best gift EVER," she breathes. "Thank you."

She runs off quickly, past me, past Lily and Amara, towards the driveway.

"See you later, alligator," her voice comes back over the wind.

"In a while, crocodile," I whisper, smiling.

Amara's eyes are burning bright into my face. A smile dawns on her face.

"When you are ready, I will be at your side. I can wait while you say your goodbyes," she speaks to me gently and patiently.

Then, she turns and walks towards the lake, her thick glowing hair fluttering in the wind behind her. As she reaches the water, her human form falls away and a bright reflection from the sun races across the water.

Exhausted, I lay down on the sand. I feel hollow and so tired.

"You found me," I say to Lily as she lies down beside me, her face close to me.

"You found yourself, Sam," she says, her voice distant.

The sun beats down on us, too bright and too hot. The wind has died down. There are bright colours caught in the tears on her face. She looks so beautiful.

"I'm sorry," I say, shaking my head, ashamed. "I'm so sorry I tried to kill you and gave everything away."

"Me, too," she says, nodding, her face full of sadness. "Me, too."

Her hand comes up to my face and covers my eyes.

My eyelids come down like a curtain.

I'm lying on the sand but the sun has fallen towards the mountains behind Peachland. Hours have gone by. It must be after dinner now.

I groan and slowly stand up. I walk to the cabin and step inside through the half-open door. The couch and rocking chair are in the room but the hearth is empty and cold.

I go back outside, confused, rubbing my forehead.

Bodie's car is nearby. The top is down and the keys are sitting in the ignition but there's no sign of him anywhere. There's a piece of folded yellow paper tucked underneath one of the windshield wipers. I pull it out and open it.

"Dear Sam," the note reads in tidy, careful handwriting. "Take the car and drive yourself home. Leave it on the street and I will come to retrieve it later. Tomorrow, you will find the car gone and the house for sale. Lily and I have left the city and we shall not be returning."

I shake my head, confused. Leaving? Now? Why?

"I know what you have become and I concur with Lily's assessment that you need time alone to understand the ramifications of your actions. Some say courage belongs to those who are only fortunate enough to accomplish a goal of which they were too dimwitted to know there was no chance to succeed. You are both brave and foolish, Sam, but I respect you nonetheless.

"You will be tempted to try to find Lily immediately.

Please resist that urge as long as you can. Be patient and wait until she rediscovers you again. It could be weeks or months or even years but your love for one another is true and it will endure. When next you meet, you will be changed and so will she. You will both be wiser and sadder, for those two states walk hand in hand.

"I look forward to our next meeting because I know you will have much to share with me. Knowledge may be my domain but I know enough to realize there are discoveries we each must make on our own, in our own way. Take this time, Sam, and use it to heal your wounds."

Bodie is trying to tell me something but I'm not getting it. My head feels stuffed with fog. I understand each of the individual words but I can't hang on to their meaning as a group. There are strands of important information dangling in front of me that I can't quite reach.

"You have responsibilities, to yourself and others. I am confident your increasing maturity will let you complete these tasks, while rising above to face what lies ahead. I apologize for my lack of clarity but it would be wrong for me to tell you more. You must write your own story. Coming here today was a first step in that process, however noble and foolhardy it was. Point the car forward and drive now to the rest of your life."

I climb into the driver's seat, laying Bodie's note on the seat beside me. I turn the key and the motor comes to life. I sigh and put the car into gear.

Bodie's note blows out of the car on a straight stretch of Lakeshore Road, once I hit the pavement and hit the gas to go faster. I see it fluttering in the air in the rearview mirror.

I keep driving.

Redemption (Lily)

Bodie and I are walking down Richter Street. The sun scorches us overhead but I ignore it for now.

"I passed the test," I say to the air in front of me. "I put his wanting over mine."

Bodie says nothing. He is staring into the distance with a troubled look. He has found the outcome unsatisfactory.

I stood by Sam when I could have killed him.

It would have been easy, just as easy as it was with Samael.

I let him choose. I forgave him.

Now he must live with his choices.

He betrayed me.

He gave his heart away to the little girl.

I still want him, even after that.

"You should stay away from him. He needs to absorb what he has done and what he has become," Bodie finally mutters.

I passed my test.

Sam failed his.

What a stupid boy.

I still want him.

"We should have a coffee together," I say as we turn a corner.

"Forget it," he replies, pulling his sunglasses onto his nose.

"Come, Bodie. It is time I spoke with her directly instead of through you," I insist, as the coffee shop comes within sight.

Two blacks (Bodie)

I bring the two of them each a huge white mug of the

darkest roast the store has available. Everyone else in the place is sipping on sweet iced beverages and these two young girls face each other with hot coffee in their hands.

They deserve no milk or no sugar. I hope they see themselves in their drinks but they are too busy studying each other to notice.

I sit back and watch and listen, a wildlife biologist staring through his binoculars as two predators circle each other, baring their teeth.

"Your time left is short, Lilith," Amara says after swallowing a huge gulp of the steaming black liquid. "You should go to him," she adds through gleaming teeth.

Lilith smiles with her lips only. She takes her own sip of coffee. "No, not yet," she replies slowly. "You can have him, for now. Get to know your creation better."

Amara places her elbows on the table with her chin in her folded hands. "You can feel how much he wants me," her words stab through the air.

Lilith imitates Amara's pose. Their faces are a short distance apart. If not for the threat in the air, they would be lovers, sharing an intimate moment in this public place.

"Eventually, he will want me back," Lilith responds coolly.

Amara shakes her head slowly. "Not for long, Lilith. Not for long at all."

Lilith leans back into her chair, grabbing her cup again and drinking most of what is left.

"That is not for you or me to decide, Amara. If it was, we would not be sitting here having this great coffee." Lilith speaks into her cup at the remaining liquid swirling in the bottom of the ceramic container.

Amara has also fallen back into her chair now and she is laughing. Some of the people in the room look over at her, startled. Her laugh is clear and high and musical but there is something off-key with it, like it is being filtered through a sound program on a computer before broadcast.

"You speak as if you were the first one to have faith in Samael but I embraced a belief in an outcome I could not control long before you," she says, finishing her coffee and standing.

Lilith does not move, except for her eyes, always on Amara.

"You have become like me. Your devotion to him will be your undoing, just as it was mine. Just because you desire a better result does not mean you shall have it." Amara's eyes are now soft and she looks at Lilith with overwhelming sympathy. "Bodie, thank you for the coffee. I always appreciate your counsel," she walks around my chair, her hand brushing the back of my neck.

"Lilith, it has been my pleasure to see you once more. You have nothing but my pity," she purrs, reaching out to touch Lilith's shoulder as she moves by.

Lilith flicks her hand up, brushing away Amara's approaching fingers as if they were flies. "You know what you can do with your pity, bitch."

It is the first and only anger I have witnessed in this entire conversation, which has now ended. Amara is walking out through the door into the daylight. She is herself again for the first time since Samael died.

Lilith, on the other hand, is not herself.

Not anymore.

She remains slumped in her chair. She holds her trembling hand in the air towards me in the hope that I will look away but I cannot.

The tears streaming down her face are hypnotizing.

The summer of my discontent (Sam)

I park Bodie's car in front of Lily's house instead. If they don't want to see me, I certainly don't want to see them. I walk home as fast as I can and make straight for my room, slamming the door.

I collapse on the bed and just lie there. I don't cry. I don't sleep. I just lie face down staring at the wall. I don't feel anything. I should be sad that Lily has run away. Bodie's note said something different but I know what's really going on. I betrayed her and she can't bear to be near me. I should be sad or ashamed but instead I just feel hollow. I killed two guardians out of pride. I gave up my heart because I didn't care.

Mom calls me for supper through the door but I just say I'm not feeling well after all my exams and want to sleep. She buys that easily. I hear her giving Sara hell later on when Sara is shouting to Mom and Dad on the other side of the house to ask if they know where her science textbook is.

"Will you keep your voice down, young lady," I hear my mom stomping from the living room. "Your brother is sleeping. He's not feeling well."

It's June so it's nearly 10 by the time the room gets dark. I walk out of my room towards the front door.

"Mom, I need some air so I'm going for a walk," I say as I walk past the kitchen. Mom is sitting at the table working on a crossword in the newspaper.

"Are you feeling better?" she calls as I open the door.

"Yeah, sure," I say as I shut it firmly.

I head straight to the lake and it's completely dark out by the time I get there. I go to the farthest end of the beach, take off my clothes except for my underwear and run into the water. It's still cold but the sharp wetness soothes my skin. I feel the dust fall off me as I dive into the blackness and swim underwater as long as I can. Only when my lungs are aching do I finally surface.

I can still stand but the water is up to my neck. Looking at the lights on the homes on the west side of the lake, standing in the cold murky water, I feel so far from this afternoon. I can't even imagine the torture Kyle and Dan put me through. What was that? Where was that?

Does it matter?

Seeing Amara and Lily and the little girl on the beach feels less like a dream and more like someone else's memory has found its way into my head. I only know I brought my heart back to life and then gave it away but not to Lily.

I'm not upset. Not at all.

I touch my neck with my hand, feeling around with my fingers for a pulse but there is none.

I close my eyes and know I can slide out of this skin right now, just by thinking about it. I can let whatever is inside me roam across the night and among the stars, finding all the guardians, and the little girl, and Amara, and Lily too.

With Amara's help, I turned my back on my human side but I'm not a guardian, either. I'm something different but I don't know what.

But the longer I stay in the water and the dark, the more relieved I feel and the further I get from this afternoon. That was an imposter who did those things. The real Sam is here and ready to get going on his life, his summer job, going to university in the fall.

Eventually, I walk back to shore. I put on my clothes over my soaking skin and take my time getting home. On my own streets, in my own house, among my family, inside my own body, I feel completely at home again, for the first time in a long time. I see myself in the mirror and I look like me. I'm not worried about who I am or what is going to happen next. I'm in the right now.

My good mood doesn't leave and my family thinks it's fake.

Mom gives me lots of sympathy, Dad gives me plenty of space and Sara gives me knowing smirks because that cool girl Lily finally came to her senses and dumped her moron brother. I tell them that Lily moved back to Vancouver to stay with her dad because this place just reminded her of Cindy. Like before, I'm able to make it feel true when the actor in my head is moving my tongue and mouth to say it.

The days go by and now it's the end of June. Pete comes around to say goodbye for the summer. His dad got him a job in northern Alberta making a stupid amount of money working in the bush at some mining camp. We play video games and I kick his butt even worse than usual but he doesn't give me grief with as much effort as in the past. It's easy to laugh and joke around and say nothing of importance around Pete because that's what he wants.

"Make sure my girl doesn't get into any trouble while I'm gone," he jokes as he leaves.

"Yeah, sure."

I haven't forgotten any of the things Cherry and Ruby showed me about myself before I killed them. I have the power to make any of those things come true. I can just stand here on the doorstep, watching Pete head away down the street and let my mind find Kathy. Instead of being at home, where Pete is going to spend his last evening with her before flying out the next morning, she would be on her way here. She would tell me with complete sincerity that

Pete is a distraction and all she ever wanted is me.

For the first time in two weeks, since I came back from Amara's cabin on the lake, I feel something. That horrible hatred I had of myself under Cherry and Ruby's eyes is there, along with an anger that fills me so fully that my throat tightens and I close my eyes to stop myself from exploding.

"I am not that person, I am not that person, I am not that person," I whisper over and over.

The feeling eventually passes but the question remains.

What are you then? It's the question I can't stop avoiding.

Amara reminds me every day what she thinks I am. It's the best summer Kelowna has seen for years, everyone keeps saying, for a place accustomed to beautiful weather. As June becomes July, the days of sunshine and heat stretch out endlessly. I can feel Amara in the sun. Her light is close and sure. She loves me and craves me. She wants me to fly into the light and there is part of me that wants to spread my wings and go to her.

I quit the comic book store, apologizing to Ted, so I can take a job with a landscaping company. I want to be outside, working my body and feeling Amara's light and warmth on me. I feel like she's touching me all the time.

Every night, I go to the beach and sit there, watching her set over the lake and the mountains. I want to go to her most then but I look back and see the sky darkening and know I don't have to. Eventually, her light fades as the day ends. I miss her but now, in the dark, I have some space to myself. In that space, I feel myself again but I feel something forming. It's still the old Sam I knew, but combined with something genuine, where I can see, where I'm not so scared. At night, alone, sitting in a chair staring out my bedroom window, because I don't need to sleep anymore, I don't want to fly to the light. I want to stay here and enjoy my sore body unused to so much physical work.

Kathy starts joining me at the beach in the evening, after she gets off her shift at the mall. She teases me about my darkening tan and how my body is getting lean and muscular from the work. I hear her laugh and look over to see her bright teeth and shining eyes. In that wonderful face, I see everything that is right about the world.

"I love you," I finally say to her one night in mid-August, taking hold of her hand.

"I love you, too, Sam," she smiles.

Then she sees me and her eyes widen. "Sam…"

"It's ok," I say. "I love you because inside you there's a jewel that never stops sparkling. It's true and it's perfect. I don't deserve to have that."

"Sam…" she protests.

"No, let me finish. It's you, here, right now, that shows me a different way. My own way. You don't see me, you see the person I want to be. You help me see that person better. You give me hope that I can get to that place. That's why I love you."

I want to tell her more but that confession and thanks has to be enough.

"Sam," she's laughing again. "What makes you think I see you any different? I could never have been with Pete if I didn't believe what I know you see in me."

I squeeze her hand tight and look across the lake. The sun is gone and I don't miss it.

"He'll be home soon," I say.

"He better be," she agrees, squeezing back.

That night, when I close my eyes, I don't have a dream but I see a place. It's on a hill and there's a city down below in the distance. There are a series of buildings nearby. At the centre of the space between the buildings, there's an oval courtyard with smooth brick stones to walk on. Lily is standing there, waiting for me. She looks cold and alone.

It's gone the instant I open my eyes.

The following nights, I see her again for just that second but then I get the slightest taste of her scent. It's different from before, not as sweet or overwhelming. It still has a fullness that makes me want to take a deep breath but it isn't as lush. It's cool and quiet, like a tree on a hilltop, offering the only shade for miles around.

I want to lie in that shade again. It's the only place I can imagine where I can rest. She knows everything about me, she sees all the weakness and cruelty, she sees the terrible things I'm capable of doing, of being, and she still believes in me. She knows I'm drawn to Amara and will never be able to be completely free of her but she still wants me.

The final days before I leave for Prince George are hard. I'm sad to be leaving Kelowna and a little nervous about heading off by myself to university but this is what I wanted. Like Dad, I wanted to be an engineer but I wanted to have a job that would help the environment somehow so this program in Prince George seems to fit. I could have gone to Vancouver but it's cheaper in Prince George and I wanted to go to a smaller school, in a smaller place.

Still, I keep seeing Lily in that courtyard. Is dreaming about her the only way I can ever see her again? Thinking about her used to make me miserable all the time. Now that feeling is not so bad. I can see a day without her. I'm not sure that's what I want but if that's what she wants, I'm ok. I won't force myself on her.

Mom's friend picks me up at the bus station after the 12-hour ride north on the Friday night before classes start at the university. Leanne chats constantly on the drive to their house in College Heights. Her husband Phillip is out of town on some business trip but will be back Sunday. She gives me a tour of the house and shows me the basement suite where I'll be living. Not much light gets down here, even during the day, but it's cozy and it has its own outside entrance so I can come and go when I want.

She finally leaves me alone and it's after midnight by the time I finish unpacking. I turn off the lights and sit but the window is too high for me to look out of without standing.

"I said I would never fight you, Sam, but I also said I would never abandon you," I hear her say again in the dark.

I can feel her hand holding mine. In that grip, I feel someone who will never let go, no matter how far I stray. On the beach, when it mattered, Lily believed in my heart even after I had given up on it. She found her humanity while I lost mine.

In the middle of the night, in a musty basement suite far from home, I feel myself walking down a sidewalk again. I hear her call Cindy a slut. I smell her for the first time as she steps off the curb and into the street towards the school.

When the room begins to turn grey, I get up and walk outside, locking the door behind me. There's already a sharpness in the air that promises a fall and winter to come. I walk up the street and hook up with Domano Boulevard. I keep walking, up the hill, past the gas stations and stores, across the traffic light at the highway, and up another hill. The clouds are close, blotting out the newly risen sun, and the air is wet but the rain stays away.

The road stretches off into the forest, running parallel to the hillside. The trees whisper among themselves in the morning air. By the time I come around a corner and read a large wooden sign that says "University of Northern British Columbia" I'm cold but I feel recharged. My hair is damp and plastered to my head.

I walk onto the deserted campus, following the road. There are two large parking lots to my right and, in the distance past them, through the grey haze, I can see some lights and buildings from the city. I recognize this place because I have seen it many times before, in my head.

I jog across the street towards what I know is just ahead.

I come around the corner, my steps slapping the bricks. I slow down and finally stop in the middle of the courtyard. There are buildings on three sides of me, with concrete steps between them, heading up towards another walkway that leads to more buildings and what looks like student residences further up the hill.

I look around but I'm alone.

I lower my head, a soft smile on my face. Lily wants me here.

The red stones are dry. Although it has been almost washed away, someone has written something in chalk near my feet. I bend down to look.

It says "Sam" and it has an arrow pointed towards the building in front of me.

I look up.

Lily is standing there, holding the door open.

I take a deep breath and taste her wonderful scent

again in the back of my throat.

"Are you going to stay out there or what?" she calls.

I stand up and start running.

No.

No, I'm not.

END

Disintegrate

Neil Godbout has a bachelor's degree in journalism from Carleton University in Ottawa and a master's degree in natural resources and environmental studies from the University of Northern British Columbia in Prince George. He won provincial and national recognition for his work during his 20 years as a reporter, editor and photographer before bolting into public relations and communications. Disintegrate is his first novel.